I *Shoulda'*
SEEN HIM
Coming 2

By: Danette Majette

Published by Life Changing Books
P.O. Box 423
Brandywine, MD 20613

Library of Congress Cataloging-in-Publication Data;
www.lifechangingbooks.net
13 Digit: 9781943174034

Dedication

Although we may not know what someone is going through, a small gesture or a kind word can make a difference in someone's life. There are so many people dealing with depression who may not feel comfortable talking to someone or they may not even realize they have a problem. If you or someone you know is suffering from depression please seek help. I did and it saved my life. This is dedicated to you.

National Suicide Prevention Lifeline 1-800-273-8255

Acknowledgments

Once again God has watched over me and given me the strength to make it through. To my mother Nellie Best, who at almost 70 years old goes out and hustles every book I put out. You are the ultimate hustler and I love you for it. To my father Melvin Hester, I'm so glad to have you in my life again.

To my spoiled rotten son Bryan Majette, I'm so proud of the man you've become. Whenever I need a laugh I can call you, when I need to cheer up I can count on your encouraging words. You have such a good heart and I'm glad that you've taken what Dubie, Aunt Wilma, Grandma and I have taught you. Keep striving and driving for the best and you can do anything you put your mind to. Love you!

To my daughter Marketa Salley, I don't know what I'm going to do when you leave and go off to married life. LOL You have taken such good care of me and pushed me to go above what even I thought I was capable of. You are such a beautiful woman on the inside and out. Love you Keekums Bear!

To Ashlie Majette and Andrea Thomas, I thank you for loving my children even when it's hard. They're definitely their mother's children. Lol. You ladies are such a blessing and I couldn't ask for better daughter-in-laws.

To my BFF Jackie Davis and my sister Shelly Majette Carrington…well we did it again! I almost lost my mind these last couple of months but thank God I have you two to encourage, push and challenge me. Thank you so much for all that you do for me. Love you!!!! To my brothers Ronald and Melvin Williams, Kevin Levy and Equan Harley, my sister-in-law Keisha Williams, Marc Salley, Brandi Salley, Betty Hamilton and my God Father Earl Taylor, I thank you guys for your support and love once again. It really means the world to me.

To Tressa "Azarel" Smallwood, thanks for all that you do.

You not only give us these amazing opportunities but you teach and guide us throughout our writing process. You are not just an amazing publisher and savvy business woman… you're an amazing friend! To Virginia Greene, I thank you for all of your help. Our early mornings and late nights have paid off. To Leslie Allen, Tasha Simpson and the rest of the LCB crew it has been a pleasure working with you guys and I look forward to our future projects. To Kellie @dzinebk thanks again for the amazing cover!

To my families…. the Majette's and the Hester's, thank you for being my biggest fans. To my girls, Sheena Smith, Vace Evans and Sabrina Wright-Young, your friendships have meant the world to me. Even though we all are living in different states, you guys are close to my heart.

Odessa Hall, Laron Profit, Malik Savage of the "Let It Flow Band", Violette Rice-Assenza, Nicole Rochelle, Danie Thomas, Michelle Butler, Travell Williams, Necole Salley, Noelle Salley, Linda Salley, Davon and Marty Salley, Andrea Doyle, Michelle Davis, Tiffany Stokes-McCaskill, Sasha Brown, Mike Kenney, Ayana Knight, Cheryl Bruce, Krystal Coleman, Michelle Parham, Alicia Moore, Lucion Freeman, Super Producer Bink Harrell, D.C. Councilman Sedrick Muhammad, Gospel Artist James "Kelly Fox" Davis, SSH Photography and my cover model, the lovely Miss Mecca.

To my friend, Craig "Chedda Diamondz" Scott from Queens, NY, it's almost that time! Be prepared to deal with me….I'm very spoiled. LOL

To Ms. Joann Davis and Mr. Sherlock McDougal at Shaw University, thanks again for helping me even when I showed up at your office without an appointment. LOL

To all of the veterans and military service men and women who have served and are serving this country, I salute you. We are truly in a league of our own. Semper Fi!!!

Smooches,
Danette Majette
P.S. Follow me!
Instagram: @dcmajette /Facebook: Danette Majette

Follow Life Changing Books:

Instagram-@lcbooks

Facebook-LCBooks

Twitter-@lcbooks

www.lifechangingbooks.net

...ONE...

Subconsciously, I could hear everything. I saw everything. All these people came to see me? Why? Why are they all crying, disheveled? Was I dying? Damn, I'm having an outer-body experience.

I could see Sheba, my mom, my brother, K-Dog but when I tried to talk nothing came out. I felt exhausted beyond belief. Please Lord, don't let me die. I know I only pray when the going gets tough but my babies need me.

● ● ●

In shock, Sheba sat in the waiting room staring at the empty chair in front of her. She listened as the nurses rolled around medical equipment and used medical jargon. Sheba was treated and released for a cut above her right eye from the scattered glass caused by stray bullets. As soon as my mother and brother arrived, they asked Sheba where I was.

"There was so much blood. I tried...I tried.... but I couldn't..." Sheba said in a trance

My brother shook her hard. "Where's Zsaset?"

When she didn't answer, he went up to the nurses' station to get some information. My mother was right on his heels.

1

While they were talking to the doctor, Vicki and Londa showed up. Vicki sat next to Sheba and tried to comfort her. "Thank God you're okay. Where's Zsa?"

"There was nothing I could do. I tried and I tried," she said crying.

After the doctor slowly broke down the news to them, my mother collapsed in my brother's arms. With a nurse's help, he walked my mother back to the waiting area and sat her down. My mother was distraught.

"What did he say?" Vicki asked.

He looked at the girls for a second then said, "He said it doesn't look like she's going to make it." He was on the brink of being in tears.

Frankie also gave them some more bad news that triggered a screaming meltdown. My mother started praying, "Father, we're going to need you more than ever. Our hearts are broken and our spirits are mourning. We pour out our hearts to you. Comfort us with your love O God. In Jesus name…amen." My mother sat shaking her legs.

"I can't believe this happened," Vicki said, wiping the tears from her face.

"That poor child. She didn't deserve this," my mother said.

"We need to call Deonte. I don't have his number though," Vicki said.

"I used to have it but he changed it," Frankie said.

Sitting crouched forward in their uncomfortable chairs, my family and friends cried and prayed as they watched the door in hopes of someone coming to tell them I was going to be alright. The stress, anxiety and uncertainty was unbearable. All that day, people came in and out of the hospital to give my family some support and well wishes.

The police showed up and tried to question Sheba about the shooting but she was still in a state of shock and able to even talk to them. They understood what she was going through, but in order to catch the shooters they had to question her. Sheba pulled herself up enough to answer some of their questions.

Two hours later, Brenda made her way to the waiting area. She suffered a few cuts and bruises from falling on the ground to cover Zeta. Frankie walked over to update Brenda. When he did, she broke out in tears.

"I shouldn't have bought Zeta home. I should've just kept her with me all day." Brenda said

She sat next to Londa who was still comforting Sheba. Vicki looked over at Brenda and said, "It's not your fault. No one could've seen this coming."

It seemed like endless hours went by as everyone gave each other support. It was the longest night ever, and they all were emotionally exhausted. But when the surgeon appeared and walked into the waiting room, they all jumped to their feet. Looking tired and grim, the scruffy looking surgeon looked at my mother and said, "We did everything we could do. She's now resting comfortably and may only receive two visitors at a time. We will notify you when her room is ready. Until then, please make yourselves comfortable as possible. We know this is a trying time for your family. Please bare with us while we try to get her well."

●●●

My mother and brother stood vigil at my bedside once I was assigned a bed. My mother's heart ached. Her once brilliant daughter who had big dreams was now replaced with a lost little girl who couldn't find her way. Her faced was streaked with tears.

Vicki and Londa took Sheba back to my house so she could get out of the bloody clothes she was in. When they returned they quietly entered my room not knowing what to expect. They hugged my mother and brother and asked about my condition.

"The doctor said she lost so much blood she needed a blood transfusion. The bullet clipped a main artery. If Sheba hadn't applied pressure to it the way they did she would've be dead," my mother told them. She gave Sheba a hug and thanked her. "They told us she might not make it and we should have everyone come say their goodbyes but I'm not accepting that." She kept stroking my hair.

"Momma, let's go down to the cafeteria and get you something to eat," Frankie said.

"No! What if she wakes up and I'm not here."

Frankie grabbed my mother's hand and said, "Mommy, you heard the doctor. She might not make it."

"He don't know my God then. My God is going to save her. We already lost one person to this. God ain't gonna take your sister, too."

Not able to persuade my mother to eat, Frankie went to get the food himself.

As the hours passed, everyone paced back and forth hoping for a miracle.

"How do you think she's gonna take the news when she wakes up?" Londa said.

Vicki shook her head. "I don't know. She was already on the brink of a breakdown. This is going to send her over the edge," Vicki said solemnly. "We're gonna have to be there for her more than ever now."

"Why would someone want to shoot her?" my brother asked.

"We don't know. Everyone loves Zsaset," Vicki said.

"So, it must've been them hoodlums she's been hanging out with."

"Hey, this is not the time. What's important now… is she's alive," my mother said, giving my brother a serious look. "She's going to need us."

"She's going to need counseling. That's the only way she's going to make it through this," Frankie said not caring who got mad.

Surprisingly, everyone agreed.

My mother kept rubbing my head then she started

singing "Still Here" by the Williams Brothers. I couldn't see her but I could hear her voice. I knew her voice from anywhere because as a child she would sing gospel songs to me all the time. In a subconscious state, I could hear the people shuffling around me but I was confused about where I was. Then I started having flashbacks of the shooting. Seeing Sheba, K-Dog, O.B and Quan lying on the ground next to me made my body jolt. It finally dawned on me that I was in a hospital and why I was there. I had been shot. *Oh my God, where is Zeta? Where are the guys?* I needed to get up. I tried with everything in me to wake up but I couldn't.

I Shoulda' SEEN HIM Coming 2

...TWO...

Three hours later, I could feel that the drugs were wearing off because I could hear people talking.

"Mama, stop crying," Frankie said.

"I need my father Jesus Christ to spare her life."

"Well, if she wasn't hanging out with thugs and drug dealers she wouldn't need saving."

"Frankie, not right now," my mom warned.

My mother's stern warning even scared Londa and Vicki. They sat quiet, not saying a word, watching my mother and brother go back and forth. Sheba had been around us long enough to know how crazy my family could get.

"Mama, that's her problem. You never hold her accountable for her actions. Every time she does something off the wall it's because daddy wasn't around. He wasn't around for me either but you don't see me getting shot at."

"I know but Zsaset took it harder than you did," my mom said.

I slowly opened my eyes. I was groggy and my sight wasn't clear but I could see another figure standing over me. It was my brother Frankie. Then three more figures. I tried to focus but my eyes felt so heavy.

"Ze…" I murmured.

"Thank you Jesus, thank you," my mother said, throwing her hands up in the air and waving them.

"Zzzzz…." I mumbled.

"What baby?" my mom asked

"Ze…Ze…," I said irritated. The alarms started to go crazy because my blood pressure was rising.

"Where's Zeta?" I managed to get out.

She ran her hands up and down my cheeks, "Shhhhh."

"Where's my baby?" I asked, trying to get out of bed, "Where is she?"

"Hey, it's okay…everything is okay," Vicki said, trying to help my mother.

"Everyone's okay?" I asked.

My mother started to cry and everyone just looked at one another. That's when I knew something was wrong. I became so upset I nearly pulled my IV out of my arm when they wouldn't answer me. The nurse came running in and immediately checked the machines I was hooked up to.

"Mrs. Jones, you have to stay calm for us, okay," the petite nurse with long blonde hair said.

"Where's Zeta? Where is she? Where is she?" I said, getting agitated again.

"Zsaset, calm down," Frankie yelled.

I tried sitting up in the bed but I couldn't. When I wouldn't settle down the nurse reached into her pocket and pulled out a syringe. She grabbed my IV bag and squeezed the contents of the syringe into my IV line. The alarms started to slowly go back to their regular sounds. I was starting to feel tired so my head hit the pillow and the whole room started to spin. "I gotta get Zeta," I said, feeling dizzy.

Londa rubbed my head. "Hey, don't worry about that right now. You need to rest."

I slowly started to drift off to unconsciousness.

● ● ●

The next morning when I woke up, K-Dog was sitting in a chair next to my bed. O.B was standing by the window.

I looked around the cold quiet room trying to get my

head straight. I instantly popped my head up, "Where is Zeta?" I said in a panic.

K-Dog quickly grabbed me and said, "Calm down. She's okay. She's at Brenda's house."

I laid back down and tried to catch my breath.

I kept opening and closing my eyes trying to get them to adjust to the light in the room. "Thank God y'all are okay. I had a dream that somebody got hurt," I said, grabbing his hand.

K-Dog had this distant look in his eyes and they were blood shot red. I assumed he had been crying because of me. I told him to raise the bed because I was uncomfortable in the position I was in. Once I was up and able to get myself together, I looked down at the bandages on my arm.

"What happened?" I asked.

"You don't' remember?" K-Dog asked softly.

I sat for a few minutes as my mind tried to catch up. "Someone was shooting at us? Why were they shooting at us?"

"We don't know but I'm going to find out." K-Dog said.

I lightly felt the bandage that was on his head. "Did you get shot, too?"

"One grazed me but I'm okay. Wouldn't be the first time," he said trying to lighten the mood.

"God, I'm in so much pain." I said in agony.

"Here, push this. It's for your pain," he said, handing me a pump.

I gave myself a hit and then started talking again. "Is Zeta okay?"

"Yeah, Brenda was able to cover her face so I don't think she saw too much. Brenda had taken her in the house by the time the police and ambulance arrived. She was a little upset when she saw Brenda bleeding."

I shook my head at the thought but I was relieved she was okay. "I'm a lousy mother."

"Don't say that. This wasn't your fault. None of us saw this comin'."

"I got to make...," was all I could get out before I was

9

out like a light.

K-Dog looked at O.B. "Is she asleep?"

O.B chuckled. "Yeah. I think so. That's what Morphine does to you."

"Damn, that's some powerful shit. We're selling the wrong stuff."

I slept for about five minutes then I started talking right where I left off. I looked around and then it hit me that Quan wasn't there. "Where's Quan?" I asked, clearing my throat.

"Oh, you're probably thirsty. Let me get you some water." He picked up the beige colored pitcher and poured me some water in a cup. He held the straw up to my lips so that I could take a sip. That sip of water tasted like a nice cold Pepsi to me. I laid my head back.

"What were we talking about?"

"I don't know but I think you need to get some rest."

"Oh, I know. Where's Quan? Is he at the house?"

Neither one said a word. They just looked at one another and then hung their heads low.

"Where's Quan?" I tried to yell but couldn't because my throat was still so dry.

Against his better judgment K-Dog decided he needed to be honest with me.

"I don't even know where to begin." He held my hand. Then he looked at O.B who turned his head and looked out of the window.

"No, he's not at the house." He took a really deep breath and started crying which scared me. "When Quan grabbed you to get you on the ground, the bullet went through your arm and…"

I felt a tightness in my throat. "And what?"

"It um…it went into his chest."

"Oh my God! He's here, too. I need to see him," I said, trying to get out of bed.

He told me to get back into bed but I wouldn't listen. "He's not here."

"Where is he?" I asked, settling down.

He looked at me for a minute before he finally said the words. "He's gone."

"What do you mean he's gone?"

"He didn't make it," he said, crying.

He sat on the edge of my bed holding me. There was such a heavy feeling in my chest.

"No…no….noooo," I cried. I was sick. "He died because of me?" I asked.

"No, he died because some bitch ass niggas were shootin' at us," O.B said huffed up.

My body was numb. I couldn't believe this had happened. I cried as K-Dog held me in his arms and comforted me.

"Who do you think it was?" I asked.

K-Dog looked at O.B. "I have my suspicions but I'm not sure just yet," he said wiping his face.

"Well, you might think you know, K-Dog…but I know it was him," O.B said, simmering.

"Who is it?" I asked getting antsy.

Before he could answer, my mom, Sheba, Brina, Vicki, and Londa entered the room. My mother kissed me and informed me that my brother had to go back to Norfolk. I wasn't surprised. He was never around when I needed him. He would put on a good act for my mom but when it came right down to it. He could've cared less whether or not I lived or died.

They walked over to my bed. "Don't ever scare us like that again," Sheba said, rubbing my hair. "Oh my God! We were so worried about you."

Brina spoke to me and rubbed my hand but she wasn't her normal self. She was very distant towards me and didn't even acknowledge K-Dog. But I couldn't focus on that.

Utterly distraught and questioning every aspect of my life, I cried and sobbed like a baby. It was my fault Quan was dead because I just froze when I saw the guns. No matter how much everyone tried to console me, I couldn't stop crying. My crying made everyone in the room start to cry. I don't think I ever knew how close Quan, K-Dog and O.B were until that moment. It was like their heart had been ripped out of their souls. I lost a good friend and father figure but they lost a brother. I was so distraught and I felt so bad for his family.

Quan and his parents were very close. I couldn't imagine what they were going through. From what I was told, Quan's dad was the leader of the Queens Southside Bloods. I knew things were about to get real because there was no way Quan's dad or K-Dog were going to sit back and let whoever did this get away with it. The city of Richmond was about to be a battlefield because there was definitely going to be a war.

K-Dog and O.B had to meet the funeral home director to discuss how to get Quan's body back to New York so they were about to leave to handle that. As they were preparing to leave, Dolo walked into my room with a dozen roses.

I could hear O.B mumble, "What the fuck he doin' here?" I turned and looked at him.

I didn't understand what all the hostility was about. Dolo sat my flowers down then gave me a kiss. "I was so worried I was gonna lose you."

K-Dog sucked his teeth then tried to play it off like he had some food stuck in his tooth.

"I'm going to be okay."

"Good," he said.

The guys gave me a hug and left while everyone else stayed and told their favorite Quan story, while Dolo just listened. I zoned out a couple of times. I wondered how long it was going to be before Detective Berry came and arrested me. I needed to make plans for Zeta when that happened. She probably would have to live with Deonte. *What the hell am I gonna do? I'm not cut out for jail.*

When visiting hours were almost over, my mom, my girls and Dolo said their goodbyes to me. Curious as to why Brina had been avoiding me, I asked her to stay a moment longer so she and I could talk. I watched as Brina pulled up a chair next to my bed.

She sat down but she could barely look me in the eyes. "Where have you been? I kept trying to call you. You even missed my birthday party. I texted you several times and you never replied."

She lowered her voice. "I know."

"So, what's going on?"

"Look, we should talk about this when you get out of the hospital."

I sat up. "If I've learned anything from this, I've learned that there may not be a tomorrow. Anyone of us can go at any moment. So, no, we're going to talk about this now."

She inhaled deeply then said, "I was a little upset and I didn't want us to fall out so I was just trying to calm down first before we spoke."

I know I was under the influence of pain medication but she wasn't making any sense at all. "Why would we fall out? What did I do?" I asked.

"You didn't do anything but the last time I was here I overheard K-Dog telling someone he loved you."

"He loved me? There must be some kind of mistake. I'm sure he didn't mean it like that." I tried to brush it off. "He probably meant he loves me like a sister."

"I don't think so. I've seen the way he looks at you."

"Woah," I said, putting my hand up. "I am not messing with him. He's like a brother to me."

"Well, I don't think he sees you as a sister anymore. That's why I lied and told you I met someone. I figured if I was out of the way you two could be together like you want to be."

"Brina, I have no interest in K-Dog other than a friend. I would never do something like that to you."

"I know but I'm telling you, he's in love with you and I just don't want to be the reason you guys aren't together."

She asked me if I had ever thought about being with him, I lied and told her no. I could tell she was relieved because her eyes lit up. I mean there were some moments of weakness like when Yaya came to visit that I felt a connection to him but I would never act upon those feelings.

"You have to promise me something," I said, grabbing her hand. "If you ever are unsure of something or feel some type of way about something…come to me. We've been friends for too long to not speak only to find out it was a misunderstanding."

She got up and gave me a hug. "I will."

My mom came back in the room one last time. "I'll be back in the morning. You need me to bring you anything?"

"Yes, I need a change of clothes. And oh…my phone. Oh my God! Do you think Mrs. Smith tried to call me about Ryan?"

"I'm not sure but I'll check. I think your phone was in the house. I'll bring it tomorrow." She tucked me in. "You get some rest," she said, giving me a kiss before she left.

The last time Mrs. Smith called me she told me Ryan didn't want to come live with me. *He's probably changed his mind by now,* I thought.

●●●

I was half asleep when I saw a dark figure enter my room. I immediately started panicking. I tried to signal for the nurse but the figure took the remote. Once my vision cleared, I thought I was seeing things. *No this bitch ain't in my room.*

"What the hell are you doing?"

"I had to come see my girl," Yaya said, dressed in hospital scrubs.

If there was any doubt before that this ratchet bitch was psychotic it was reaffirmed at that moment. I looked around for something to throw at her ass and when I reached for the pitcher of water next to my bed she said, "You don't wanna do that. See, I'm the only person standin' between you and a jail cell."

I laid back. "What the hell are you talking about now? I am so sick of your ass!"

She shook her head. "Now is that anyway to talk to Yaya?"

I closed my eyes and started to pray.

"What chu doin'?" she asked confused.

"I'm praying your ass away." I tried to hold it together and thankfully the medicines were keeping me calm.

"Zsa, girl you is too funny...but look seriously, you need to pay up if you don't want our favorite detective to come and arrest yo' ass."

"Our favorite detective?"

"Oh yeah, girl! Yaya got Detective Berry in her back pocket." She sat down at the end of my bed. "Now I saw yo' momma when she left here and she don't look too good. I would hate for her to tap out because her 'lil princess got hauled off to jail.

I sat up quickly but I had to lay back because the pain was so unbearable.

"Bitch, what did you think you was gonna do? Ain't yo' ass down one arm?"

I settled back in my bed and thought about what she said. My mom would be devastated if I got arrested and her health probably would deteriorate. I didn't really have any money but she didn't know that so I lied.

"So, look, when should I pick up the $5,000?"

"Are you crazy, bitch? You see me laid up in the hospital? How in the hell am I going to get you that amount of money by next week?"

"You figure out, Zsa! Not my problem you and your crew got shot up."

"Yaya, maybe you did have something to do with it, you greedy bitch. I will get you some money and then I want you to leave me alone."

Yaya paused at my comment, allowing me to slip back in to a deep sleep but quickly came to when Yaya started to speak.

"Oh Yaya ain't gon' never leave you alone, baby. No...no...no, this is only the beginning of our 'lil arrangement, believe me. I need you to do something else for me but we'll discuss that at a later time."

"Why are you doing this?" I asked growing more and

more frustrated by the second. I could not figure out her game and this was one game I did not need to play. Yaya had it out for me and I had to bring my A-game for this crazy chick.

"Where the hell do I start? She started tapping her head. "Oh yeah, now I remember. First…biiiitch you were fuckin' my damn husband. Second, you tried to poison me and third you and your 'lil girlfriend tried to clown me when I was at your house."

I guess she was referring to me putting Miralax in her soda. I would hardly call that poisoning her. I needed the nurse to come in and give Yaya's ass a shot of something. She was acting crazy times ten.

"Oh yeah, you tried Yaya, but that's okay. Cause I got yo' ass right where I want you." She stood up and walked closer to me. I thought she was going to hit me and there was nothing I could do. One arm had an IV attached to it and my other arm was bandaged. I was helpless.

"I'ma let you get some rest, okay. Here's your 'lil remote. If you need the nurse just push the red button sweetie." Before she left she looked at me and laughed. "I'll need that money next week, sucka!"

I was in shock but everything was hazy. *Did Yaya really just come in here? She is still on this blackmail shit. Oh, what was next? I knew O.B better be ready to get an earful from me. His wife was really tripping. Why was she not blackmailing Cindy, O.B's new fling?*

I had just found out the reason why Detective Berry hadn't been by to arrest me and I had just made a deal with the devil. I grabbed my morphine pump and gave myself a hit because I needed the sleep now more than ever. I had a feeling I was going to have a lot of restless nights when this was all said and done.

...THREE...

I was released from the hospital a week after I was admitted. My mom and Vicki had taken Zeta over to Brenda's while I was incapacitated. Brenda was gracious enough to take care of her in spite of almost being shot herself. I was anxious to see Zeta but I needed a day or two more to get myself together. As soon as I walked in the house, I felt something was wrong. I thought it was anxiety because I was back at the place of the shooting but that wasn't it. Tired, I shook it off and made my way to the couch. I was in so much pain I wanted to die. I reached in my purse and grabbed my bottle of water and my bottle of Percocets. Needing an update on Ryan, I called Mrs. Smith. As usual, it went to her voicemail, so I left her a message asking her to give me a call back. I was sure Ryan was over whatever it was that made him say he didn't want to stay with me. Or at least, I hoped he had. I couldn't understand how a child his age got to make the decision of where he wanted to live. It wasn't like I was abusing him. Sure, I wasn't the best mother in the world but I was doing my best.

"Hey, are you doing okay? There's a bunch of mail for you right there on the coffee table," Cindy said, in the kitchen making a sandwich.

I was a little irritated that she was acting so nonchalant like nothing happened. But then again we weren't the best of friends so what did I expect.

"Okay." I took my medicine first then went through the mail. It was all the normal stuff like bills, advertisements and flyers but one piece of mail stood out.

"This has both our names on it," I said, holding it up.

"Oh yeah, I had to sign for it. I wanted to wait until you got home before I opened it."

It was a certified letter from Richmond Civil General Court. For a minute, I thought it was a warrant but it said civil and my case would have definitely been in Circuit Court. I held the envelope with my injured arm and opened it with my other arm. Once it was unfolded, I carefully read the document.

"What the fuck?" I yelled.

"What happened?" Cindy asked, coming into the den.

I dropped the letter and started to cry. "What am I gonna do now?" She stood over me scanning the document. "They'll never give Ryan back to me."

"What does this mean?"

"I don't…," I couldn't even finish my sentence. I started having heart palpitations. I felt lightheaded and queasy. Before I could get up and run to the bathroom, I had vomited all over the floor. Cindy grabbed some paper towels and handed them to me. I asked her to quickly grab my water because my throat felt irritated. She told me to sit as she picked the bottle up and handed it to me. I took a few sips then sat with my head in my hand.

"Look, we'll just go to court and straighten this whole thing out," she said, putting her arms around me trying to get me to relax. It didn't work so she told me to go get cleaned up and get in bed and she would clean up my mess. I thanked her and made my way up to my room. I cleaned up as best I could then laid in my bed. My muscles were so tense and my head began to pound. *This can't be my life,* I thought. I felt like I was doomed.

As if I didn't have enough problems, my apartment complex had filed eviction papers against us. They claimed we were involved in illegal activity that led to a shooting causing an unsafe environment for the other residents. This day had gone worse than I ever expected and just that fast. And it was about to get even more off the hook.

For the next few days, I was so depressed, I had isolated myself from my friends. I wasn't picking up my phone except if it was K-Dog. I couldn't eat or sleep. Between getting shot, the situation with Ryan and now being faced with eviction, I just felt like it would be easier if I just didn't wake up one morning.

One evening, Cindy came home and found me on the couch passed out from drinking and taking painkillers.

"Zsaset," she yelled, slapping me in the face. "Wake up."

"I'm up...I'm up," I said slurring.

"How many of these pills did you take?"

I looked at the pill bottle and laughed. "I don't know. Just two, I think. Who cares? I should be dead just like Quan is dead," I said crying.

Cindy sat me up on the couch and hugged me. "You don't mean that."

I pulled away. "Yes, I do. You just don't know how many lives I've ruined."

"Look, maybe you should just tell me everything that's going on with you. I bet if you just talk about it and get it off your chest you'll feel better," she said, sitting closer to me and placing her hand on my knee. "Just let it out."

"Maybe you're right. I've just been holding in so much and I don't know what to do. I don't know who to trust anymore. I'm just a mess."

"Okay, well start with whose life you ruined."

I took a deep breath. "Quan is dead because of me."

"That's not true. So, what else is going on with you?"

"Well, when I first got here O.B and I were..."

My phone rang and it was K-Dog. I wasn't sure if I was ready to talk to him yet. I still felt awkward about him telling someone he loved me but it could've been important so I answered it. When I looked over at Cindy she looked frustrated.

"Hey. You okay," K-Dog asked.

I lied and said, "Yes."

"Okay well, I know you're going through a lot but don't talk to no one; I mean no one. You got it."

"Yeah but why? What's going on?" I said worried, looking at Cindy's face.

"Zsaset, this is important. Don't speak to anyone until I get back."

"Okay, I understand that, but why?" I said.

"Until we find out for sure who was blazin' at us we can't trust no one. Not even Cindy's ass."

"Surely you don't think…," I looked at Cindy and she was right in my mouth.

"I don't know what to think but I think we need to be safe rather than feel sorrowful later. Stay in the house. Don't go out for nothin'. If you need somethin' let Cindy go get it. Now get some rest I'll see you when I get back," he said, before hanging up the phone.

Cindy wanted to resume our conversation but my phone rang again. You could tell by her facial expressions that she was exasperated.

"Just let it ring. You seem even more stressed after that call."

I looked at the screen. It was Dolo so I let it go to voicemail.

"So, do the police have any leads on who shot you?" Cindy asked.

"No, not yet.

"I wonder how this is going to affect their business."

Why the hell was she so concerned about their business? "Their business is none of my business so I don't know nor do I care." Cindy was making everyone's business hers.

K-Dog warned me not to talk to anyone so I told her I wasn't feeling well and needed to go lay down. Her insistence we keep talking had me looking at her sideways. *I gotta watch this bitch.* Cindy kept talking but I shut her and the conversation down then I drug myself up to my room, took a hot shower and got in the bed.

• • •

I got up early that Saturday morning. It was very cloudy outside and the forecast called for rain so I wanted to go get Zeta from Brenda's and get back in the house before it started. It seemed that whoever shot me wasn't coming back, so I thought it was safe enough to bring her back home. I brushed my teeth, reapplied some fresh bandages to my wound, threw on some sweats and headed out the door. As I drove to Brenda's, I kept mulling over the shooting and being blackmailed by Yaya. I had totally underestimated Yaya. She was actually smarter than I thought she was. I just had to find a way to be smarter.

I pulled in front of Brenda's house and put my car in park. I walked up to the door constantly looking around to make sure no one had followed me. I was becoming more and more paranoid by the minute. I started to have second thoughts about Zeta coming home but I missed her so I knocked on the door and waited for someone to let me in. When Zeta saw me she raced from the kitchen into my arms.

"Mommy…mommy!" She wanted me to pick her up but I couldn't so she settled for a hug.

"Hello Zeta Bear. You ready to come home."

"Yaaaayyy," she screamed.

"Hey. I'm glad to see you're feeling better," Brenda said.

"I'm doing better physically, but emotionally I still have a ways to go."

"That's understandable." Brenda told Zeta to go upstairs and get her things.

"I'm really sorry you got caught up in what happened at my place."

"Zsaset, it wasn't your fault." She hugged me. "Do the police have any leads yet?"

"No, that's what so frustrating. I'm not sure if it was just a random shooting or if they were actually after us. I can't for the life of me understand why anyone would be shooting at us."

That was not completely true as I thought back to the Mosby Court shootings.

"Well, hopefully they get them off the streets soon."

Before Zeta came back downstairs, Brenda whispered to me that she had been acting up.

"What was she doing?" I asked.

"Well, she said the F word."

"The F word?"

"Ummm...she said 'fuck you' to one of the other kids." Brenda said embarrassed.

"Zeta?" I asked surprised.

"Yes. She also hit another little boy I was keeping in the head because he took her toy."

I apologized to Brenda for Zeta's behavior and told her I would speak to her about it.

"I'm not trying to suggest anything but is everything okay at home? Sometimes kids act out like this when...," I raised my eyebrow. "Well, maybe she's just a little tired today." Brenda knew Zeta's home life was screwed up but she was trying to give me the benefit of the doubt.

"Maybe she is," I said, feeling myself about to curse her out.

I knew what Brenda was hinting at and even though I didn't want her implying it, she was right. She had witnessed me fighting with both Deonte and O.B and I got shot in front of her. How much could a child take after witnessing all that?

Running down the stairs with her backpack, I looked at my child and saw that I had taken away her innocence with all of my drama. That poor girl had two unstable people as parents.

We said our goodbyes and walked to my car.

On our way home, I had a talk with Zeta and explained to her that even though she heard mommy say bad words she shouldn't and she should never hit anyone. Her little face was sad as she said, "Sorry mommy." *Where was her father when I needed him?*

"It's alright, baby. Just don't do it again, okay?"

"Okay," she said, playing with her doll.

When we returned home, I told Zeta to go to her room and take a nap. I wasn't used to being home on the weekends, so I just laid on the couch and watched Netflix all day. When Cindy came home she sat on the couch and watched television with me. Later that night, Dolo showed up unannounced. Even though she had been around him before, Cindy seemed a little nervous that he was there. She kept talking about absolutely nothing and shaking her legs. Then she abruptly left. As soon as she left, Dolo suggested we go up to my room. He said I looked tired. To be honest, I was.

Snuggled up in my bed, Dolo kept telling me how glad he was that I was okay. As a matter of fact, he had become very clingy. I wasn't with that shit but with Quan gone and K-Dog's business is shambles, I needed someone to help with my car note so I had to keep Dolo close and he was happy about it. Almost too happy. Maybe he was scared the people who shot me might come back. I mean it even dawned on me too that they could come back but I didn't think they would be that stupid. Luckily for me, my new neighbor was a cop and he always bought his patrol car home and parked it right outside our door.

Dolo might've been happy but I can tell you someone who wasn't happy these days; K-Dog. His supplier was Quan's dad and after Quan's death, his father blamed K-Dog for his son getting killed so he stopped supplying K-Dog. That's why K-Dog ended up staying in New York after Quan's funeral. He needed to find another supplier and quick.

I was in a deep sleep after taking a Percocet for my pain when my phone starting ringing loudly. Dolo woke up and looked over thinking it was his phone.

"Zsa, your phone," he said, still groggy.

"Let it ring."

"What if it's your mom or your son?"

I jumped up and reached over to my nightstand and grabbed it quickly. To my dismay it was Deonte's worrisome ass. In true fashion, he had been annoying the hell out of me ever since I got home from the hospital.

"Hey, it's Deonte. Please don't hang up.Can we talk?"

"Talk about what? You fucking Nicole? No thanks."

Dolo snapped his head towards me. He was all frowned up like I was talking to him.

"Look, I'm sorry. Can we just sit down and talk about this?"

"Deonte, go to hell. Sit down with that! As a matter of fact, I wish your ass would just die," I yelled, then hung up, still immature as ever.

I slung my phone across the room in a fit of rage. Trying to calm down and looking for reassurance, I laid my head on Dolo's chest but he slid away from me.

"What's wrong with you?" I asked confused. It wasn't like I sat on the phone and had a whole damn conversation with Deonte.

"Why is your ex callin' you?" he asked.

"I don't know. I think he was trying to get back together or something but he has to know that shit ain't happening."

He got up out of the bed and slipped his Polo boxer briefs on and then his jeans. "Look, if you and that nigga gettin' back together let me know somethin'. You ain't gonna have me out here in the streets lookin' crazy."

I didn't even have the energy to fight with his ass because if I did I would've told that mothafucka a thing or two. When I didn't fall on my knees and beg him to stay, he grabbed his keys off my dresser and strolled out the door.

I guess I'll have to turn that Benz in soon because I'll be damned if I'm gonna kiss a nigga's ass anymore in life, I thought to myself as I pulled the covers over me and got comfortable. *That nigga can drink bleach and die for all I care.*

Two hours later, guess who bought their ass back to the crib? Mr. Bipolar himself.

"Dolo, I don't know what the hell is going on with you and why you left that way, but I fought with my ex for years and

I'm not doing that shit anymore. I got enough to worry about. Like people shooting at me, for instance."

"You right, Ma. I just got upset thinkin' bout losin' you."

"I'm not going anywhere. Promise," I said, kissing him on the lips.

He grabbed me and pulled me close. "Ooooo," I screamed.

"Damn, I forgot. I'm sorry."

He started kissing me, which got me moist although I did not want to be at that given moment.

"It's okay," I said, trying to remove Dolo's pants. My arm was still a little weak so I needed help and of course he was more than willing to oblige. Once his pants were off, I took him in my mouth. After a few strokes with my good hand and my tongue rotating on his raging rock hard chocolate stick, I pulled him close and turned my body around. He entered me forcefully, forgetting I was still in pain.

"I'm sorry. You okay," he asked trying to be gentle.

"Yeah, I'm fine."

He was pounding away as I contracted my vaginal muscles, driving him absolutely crazy. The sounds of love-making drifted through the thin walls as well as the rhythmic sound of the headboard slamming into the wall.Our skins slapped together until I felt a tingle shoot though my body. I yelled, "I'm cominggggg!" as I reached my orgasm. It wasn't much longer before Dolo's breath grew ragged and his eyes began to roll into the back of his head as he released inside of me.

"Damn, you got some good pussy!" he said, stroking my hair, collapsing beside me in bed. "You sure you okay?"

"Yes, please stop asking me that," I said getting irritated.

After we made love, Dolo reached down on the floor. "Here."

"What's this for?"

"I told you before you needed a gun."

I didn't want to have a gun in the house but after what happened to me I wasn't going to argue with him.

I took the Kel Tec 9mm and inspected it. It was small but it was enough to drop someone if I needed to. Hiding it in a shoebox, I then put the box on the top shelf of my closet out of Zeta's reach.

"Has anyone been talking about what happened?" I asked, getting back in the bed, knowing K-Dog told me not t speak to anyone about the circumstances.

"Naw, the streets ain't sayin' too much?"

"I can't believe someone wanted me dead."

"They didn't want you dead. They wanted your brothers dead."

I almost broke my neck when I turned my head in his direction. "How do you know that?" I asked with my eyes squinted.

He turned his body to me. "Look, when you in the streets like we are… you always gonna have someone who wants to get back at you for somethin' or take over your blocks. That's just how it is in the game. You just happened to be in the wrong place at the wrong time."

"I don't know. I just feel like it was personal."

"Well, you don't have anythin' to worry bout that cause I'm here and I'm not goin' to let anyone hurt you," he said, running his hands across my face.

I settled myself in his arms and rested. It felt good to know I had someone there to protect me even though he would have never been my first choice if my world was not crumbling around me. The question was who was going to protect me from myself because you would think getting shot would've given me a whole new perspective on life but it didn't. I made several more mistakes before it was all said and done.

...FOUR...

Two days later, I was at home drinking my sorrows away. Zeta was in her room playing. Brenda was slowly backing away from me. My guess was her husband told her to stay away from me because I was too dangerous to be around. Not to mention, Zeta was behaving very badly every time she went over there so Brenda wasn't exactly thrilled to keep her like she used to.

Laying on the couch in a black short sleeve sweatshirt, leggings and my hair pulled back in a ponytail, I tried to retrace the path of when my life fell apart. I was able to pinpoint the exact time just as my mind started to drift off. It was when I got kicked out of the Marines. I wanted to blame everyone else for my getting kicked out but truth be told it was my anger that got me kicked out. I just couldn't understand why I was so angry. Even though my father wasn't around I still had strong male figures in my life, like my uncle.

I sat up, flicked the cigarette lighter and lit a Newport I had pulled out of the box. I took a long pull and blew it out. My hands were shaking so bad the cigarette almost fell. I never felt so helpless and I was tired of looking over my shoulder and trying to keep up with all of the lies. A thought ran across my mind that I should just go to the police station and tell them the truth. I killed those guys in self-defense so maybe they wouldn't even press charges against me. This would stop Yaya from holding it over my head. She was calling my phone nonstop for days, and it was only a matter of time before she showed up at my door demanding her money that I didn't have. This madness had to stop, I was emotionally and physically a mess and I just wanted to be at peace. Even if it meant going to jail.

That evening, K-Dog, O.B and Coley showed up after they returned from New York. I hadn't seen them since I was released from the hospital so we had a lot to catch up on. The friction between them was so obvious. I didn't understand how Coley and O.B didn't know that Lina and Yaya were sisters. Especially O.B, he was married to Yaya and I'm quite sure Lina was at the wedding. As soon as they sat down, I lit into them.

"So, why didn't y'all tell me Lina and Yaya were related?"

Coley looked straight at O.B and you could tell he didn't want to throw him under the bus. However, he was also smart enough to know that if he lied to K-Dog he was going to have an even bigger problem than O.B being pissed at him. Coley bit his bottom lip then said, "O.B introduced me to Lina. I had no idea she was Yaya's sister." He looked at O.B to corroborate his story but O.B just sat there with this ridiculous look on his face.

"Come on, God! Say something," K-Dog yelled.

"What the hell you want me to say? I didn't think it mattered who was who. Hell, I didn't think they were even gonna work out. I thought he would smash and move on."

"Son, that's bullshit and you know it," K-Dog countered.

"So, is she still blackmailing you like she's blackmailing me?" I asked.

K-Dog's head swung around. "Who blackmailing who?"

All I could do was shake my head. I didn't know what the hell was going on with O.B but he was digging his own grave with all these secrets. With the cat already out of the bag, I went ahead and filled K-Dog and Coley in on what was going on. I told them how Detective Berry told me that Lina snitched and how Yaya was using that and something else to hold over O.B.

"Well, we have an even bigger problem. That bitch Yaya showed up in my hospital room trying to shake me down now. She's been working with Detective Berry and if I don't pay her she's going to have him arrest me." It was like I had sucked the air out of the room. O.B rolled his eyes, plopped his body against the wall and held his hands over his face. "She wants me to do something else but she said she'll tell me that later."

"Yo, O.B you got to do sumthin' bout her," Coley said.

"This bitch is gonna make me go crazy," I said. "It's been one thing after another since I moved here."

"That's why I said I think you need to go back to Norfolk," K-Dog said.

"Norfolk has jails, too. I just need to stay here and deal with whatever happens. I'm not about to bring this drama to my mother's doorstep."

K-Dog didn't like it but I knew it was an argument he wasn't going to win.

"We just need to figure out a way to keep her quiet," Coley suggested.

"The only way to keep her quiet is to pay her and she probably still won't keep her trap shut."

"Coley, Lina was your responsibility. That bitch snitched to the police and Yaya so you know what you have to do." K-Dog was adamant about that.

Coley shook his head to acknowledge that he understood. "What about Yaya?" I asked.

"I don't want nobody touchin' her until I find my son," O.B said. His whole demeanor changed.

"Son, I understand you want to find your seed but time is tickin'. So, you better find him quick. That bitch is about to ruin everything I've worked my ass off for. On top of that, we got niggas blazing at us. They shot Zsa and killed Quan. It's only a matter of time before they try it again unless we strike them first."

"I heard it was Dolo's boys," O.B said.

I couldn't believe he was trying to blame Dolo for this

shit.

"Dolo would never have somebody shoot me. He has no reason to. He loves me and Zeta."

K-Dog shifted his body. "I didn't know y'all were that serious." K-Dog didn't know that Dolo was just around for me to use.

Wanting to prove O.B wrong I said, "We are and he would never hurt me like that."

Something changed in K-Dog's expression. "Zsaset, what do you really know about him?"

"I know he wouldn't shoot me and kill my brother. I mean that is what he thinks anyway. That y'all are my brothers." I took the last sip of my drink. "Besides, he's been trying to find out who's behind the shooting, too." I almost didn't believe the words coming out of my mouth.

They all looked at one another as if they didn't believe me either.

"I can't say that it was him but I can't say that it wasn't him."

My eyes widened in disbelief. "I'm telling you you're wrong about Dolo."

"Maybe I am," K-Dog.

I got so pissed I got up and made myself another drink.

"Don't you think you need to slow down with all that drinkin'?" O.B asked.

"Don't you think you need to mind your own damn business?"

He just smirked at me.

I made my way back to the couch and continued to drink. As we continued our conversation, Cindy walked in. "Shhhh," I whispered. That tabled the whole conversation until another time.

"Hey, what y'all up to?"

"I'm having a drink. I don't know what the hell they doing." I said, slurring by this time.

She walked over to O.B and gave him a kiss. That was

the most uncomfortable kiss I had ever seen in my life.

"Trouble in paradise?" I asked.

"Why don't you mind your damn business now?" O.B said snapping at me.

"Touche' bitch!" I said, raising my glass.

K-Dog and Coley both laughed.

"Well, I'm about to go the house and get some sleep," K-Dog said, as he stood up.

"Coley, go with Dog and I'll pick you up when I'm done here," O.B said.

Outside, K-Dog and Coley were having their own conversation.

"I don't know what it is about that chick but I don't trust her," K-Dog told Coley.

"I don't either, God. I swear I've seen her before, though. I just can't recall where," Coley added.

"O.B in there breakin' up with her now."

"Word?"

"Yeah, we can't afford to have any more disloyal mothafuckas around. I don't know why but I feel like he ain't tellin' us everythin' that's goin' on between him and Yaya."

"You know I would've told you if I knew they were sisters. I swear, I did not know."

"I know you didn't. I'm just not buyin' why O.B never mentioned it or the blackmail. But why?"

"I don't know," Coley said, shaking his head.

"Me neither. But, first things first. We need to find Lina and Yaya."

"I know exactly where she is. Don't worry, I got plans for her ass."

"And I'm going to take care of Yaya's ass. I don't give a fuck what O.B says," K-Dog said as they drove out of my complex.

With everyone finally gone, I sat back on the couch with a freshly poured glass of liquor. It seemed to be the only thing that was numbing my pain. Not just my physical pain but my emotional pain. The emotional pain of losing Quan and feeling like my life was a train wreck. I tried to force my mind to focus on anything but the craziness surrounding me but it wasn't working.

Around five p.m., my eyelids were starting to get heavy. I decided to take a nap so I headed up the stairs. When I got to my room my cellphone rang. When I saw who it was, I shook my body to try and wake up. I was so anxious, I almost hit decline call by mistake.

"Hello," I answered.

"Hello Ms. Jones," she said, not sounding too happy.

"I'm glad you called Mrs. Smith, how is Ryan doing?"

"He's doing very well and we want to keep it like that."

I felt like she was giving me shade but I couldn't say anything to her because she held my future with Ryan in her hands.

"So, do you know when he'll be able to come stay with me?"

"Like I told you before he doesn't want to come live with you and to be honest I have to agree with him." She exhaled. "I'm very concerned about the shooting that took place at your residence.

How the hell does she know about that? "I can assure you I was an innocent bystander."

"Ms. Jones, you may have been an innocent bystander as you say but the shooting still involved people you're associated with. With that said it is my duty to keep Ryan safe so I'm placing him permanently with the foster family he's been staying with."

"Ms. Smith, please if you just give me a chance, I can prove to you that he's safe here."

"Ms. Jones, I've given you more than enough chances. I'm sorry."

I didn't hear anything else she said after that because I dropped my phone and started balling. My son was going to be cared for by strangers and there was nothing I could do about it.

Sitting stone-faced, I picked up the almost empty bottle of Vodka I had sitting on the nightstand next to my bed and threw it at the wall spazzing out. Crying off and on for an hour, I made the dreadful call to my mother to let her know what Mrs. Smith said. I wasn't sure if I should tell her because she wasn't doing really well health wise and my getting shot didn't help matters.

As soon as my mother said my name I could hear my brother in the background yelling, "What she got herself into now?"

"Tell him to shut the hell up! I can't stand his ass," I yelled back.

"I want both of you to shut the hell up." My mother must've really been tired of us fighting because I had never heard her curse before.

"I just called to tell you what Mrs. Smith said." I was quiet for a second.

"Well…what she say?"

When I told her the news about Ryan, she immediately started to blame herself for all of this happening. The next thing I knew, I heard a loud thump and Frankie yelling, "Mommy."

"Hello! Hello! Momma!"

"She fainted! I gotta call you back!"

...FIVE...

Although I wasn't 100 percent yet, I decided to go back to work a month later. With K-Dog's business up in the air, I needed the money to pay my bills and help my mother with hers. After she passed out and was taken to the hospital she was put on additional medications which were costing her a fortune. I didn't want to have to rely solely on Dolo for bill money because his ass swayed any way the wind blew. One day, he loved me to death; the next day he was mad about something. I didn't have time for the bullshit so I needed to make my own coins. Especially with my Benz car note. That's what I got for trying to live like the Jones'.

When I pulled into the parking lot near the store, I couldn't find a spot. I forgot the mall was having a back-to-school fashion show that morning. I drove over to the side closest to the food court since the store was only a few doors down and parked. Touching up my make-up, I was surprised to see Cindy talking to Dolo in the parking lot. I watched their body language and it appeared they were disagreeing about something. *Well, what do we have here? Looks to me like a little backstabbing is going on.* I still had about twenty minutes before we opened so I continued to sit in my car and watch them. But then I came up with a better plan. I stepped out of my car wearing my new Lebron's and headed straight towards them.

You would've thought Cindy was looking at Jesus Christ

himself when she saw me. She got all flushed and nervous.

"Hey, what's up?" I asked.

Moving her hair out of her face she said, "Nothing much. I ran into Dolo. So, I was just standing out here talking to him."

He tried to divert my attention by giving me a kiss.

"Ummm… so what y'all got to talk about? What y'all friends now?" I asked.

"Yo, why you trippin? I ran into her we started talkin' bout how well you doin' and how it could've been worse."

"Yeah, whatever nigga."

As soon as I said that, he told Cindy he would talk to her later.

"What the fuck do you mean you'll talk to her later?"

"I was talking to you."

"Nigga, you ain't slick," I yelled. I stared his ass down as he pimped to his car. Then I turned back to Cindy.

"He sure was in a hurry to leave. Was it something I said? And why did he say he'll talk to you later?" I asked.

"He meant you. Zsaset, I think you're reading too much into this."

"First of all, don't tell me what I'm thinking cause you have no idea what I'm thinking right now."

"Okay, I'm sorry," she said, backing up.

"I better not find out y'all messing around. Cause if I do both of y'all gonna get stabbed."

I was so mad I just walked away to the food court entrance. *She's lucky I need her half of the bills,* I thought. When I turned around I saw her drive off in her car. *Oh, so this bitch ain't even have to work today. So, this wasn't a little impromptu visit. Why were they meeting here? Is this bitch trying to get at my man because O.B dumped her? As a matter of fact she has been acting funny since then.* Whatever the case, I was going to be on her neck from now on. Maybe Londa and Vicki were right about Cindy. Maybe there was something up with her. But like my mother always told me. *"Keep your friends close and your enemies even closer."* So I was going to make it my business to find out what Cindy was up to and let K-Dog know what I saw.

• • •

Tapping on the glass door for someone to let me, I noticed we had a lot of new hot merchandise. They had even remodeled. As soon as Larry saw me he started smiling. He unlocked the door, and gave me hug.

"Oh, I'm sorry. I didn't hurt you, did I?"

"No, I'm good. It still hurts a little but it's nothing my pills can't handle," I said laughing.

"It's so good to have you back. Maybe these girls will start selling now," he said annoyed.

I walked to the back and placed my purse and jacket down on his desk.

"Oh, bring your stuff back here. They put a cabinet back here for you guys to put your stuff in so I can have my desk back."

When I saw the cabinet, my eyes rolled to the back of head.

"Larry!" I stood with my hands on my hips. "What the hell is this mess?"

"It's a cabinet."

"No…it looks like somebody stole this crap from a dumpster and put it in here." I walked my ass right back up to his desk and placed my stuff back down. He didn't say anything. He just scratched his head and went back up to the front to open the doors for business.

By lunchtime, Vicki showed up for her closing shift. "Girl, it is so good to see you back here. Larry has been getting on our damn nerves. He don't act like that when you're here."

"That's because he knows he'll get cursed the fuck out, hunty!"

We laughed and gave each other a hug. Vicky was there for me throughout this whole mess. She would sit with me in the house when I just wanted to die because I didn't feel like living anymore. I kept thinking that if this was how my life was going to be from now on then there was no use in living. I wasn't living anymore; I was just existing. But even existing was depressing for me. I would pray at night for God to just take me but then I would think about my babies. Who was going to be there for them? And I knew that it would literally kill my mother.

I took an hour lunch. Before I went back to the store, I walked over to McDonald's to ask them if Cindy was working today. I got the shock of my life when they told me she had quit a few days ago. In a daze, I made my way back to the store. *What the hell was going on?*

As I walked back to the store, I tried to come up with a plausible reason as to why Cindy had quit her job and not told me. I was running different scenarios through my head when I spotted the guy with the scar standing near the store. As soon as he saw me he turned and walked away. I pulled out my cell-phone to call K-Dog. As I was dialing his number, I quickly ran in the store and straight into two detectives wearing long trench style overcoats. One was white and one was black. I whisked past them hoping they were shopping but my hopes were dashed when Vicki told me they were waiting to speak to me. I felt my body almost shut down. Everywhere I turned there was the guy with the scar, Yaya, somebody shooting me or me shooting someone. I didn't know how much more I could take before I completely lost my mind. Maybe I was already losing my mind.

"Zsaset, you okay. Zsa...," I heard Vicki yell.

"Umm…what? What did you say?"

"Are you okay?"

"Yeah…yeah I'm fine."

I shook my hands to relieve the tension that was building up. *That bitch Yaya didn't even give me a chance to get the money.* I paced. *Calm down, maybe they're here about me getting shot. Yeah, that's it.*

My nervousness turned to embarrassment when I walked back on the floor and was asked by the detectives to come outside the door. This was the second time the police had been there. I could only imagine what Larry was thinking. He was probably going to fire me this time. No one wants the police lingering around their place of business.

As soon as I took a seat on the bench outside the store they showed me their badges. They weren't Richmond detectives. They were from Norfolk. My heart started to race even faster than it was before.

"What's going on?" I asked, about to jump off the bench. "Is my mother okay?"

"Ma'am, were not here about your mother." They looked at one another like they hated to tell me the reason they were there. Their hesitation had me holding my breath.

"Ma'am, we regret to inform you that your husband and female companion by the name of Nicole Rodgers were found dead last night."

I sat numb for a few minutes before Vicki came over and wrapped her arms around me. I was speechless as she brushed my hair back with her hand.

"How could this have happened?" I cried.

Vicki sat next to me gently rocked me. "I'm so sorry, Zsa."

I wiped my face and asked the detective what happened to them. When he told me that they had been murdered, I clutched my chest. "What? I don't understand."

"They were both shot execution style."

I told them I needed to go because I could feel my lunch about to come up.

"Ma'am, we're sorry to have to do this but we need to ask you a few questions," he said, pulling out a small note pad and pen from his shirt pocket.

"I…I don't know anything about this. We were estranged so we really didn't talk that much." At this point, I was hyperventilating and one detective was trying to calm her down.

"When was the last time you two spoke?"one of them asked.

"It's been weeks. He wanted to sit down and talk

but...I...I," I couldn't get it out.

"We talked to a few people who said you attacked them a few months ago."

I cut my eye at him. "He was sleeping with one my best friends. Yes, we got into an argument but I didn't attack them."

He jotted down a few notes then asked me if I knew who would want them dead.

"No, I don't," I said with certainty.

"Well, you told him you wished he were dead."

"I didn't mean it, literally. I was on pain meds and he was aggravating me," I said in almost a whisper. *How the hell did they know about that?*

He asked me where I was the night before between six and nine p.m. I told him I was at home with my roommate. As a matter of fact, I had gone over to Brenda's to drop Zeta off so I wouldn't have to do it before I came to work that morning. I even stopped at Food Lion to get her some Lunchables. The black detective shot me a look like he didn't believe me. I wasn't about to do his job so I said, "If you don't believe me check my cellphone activity and the security footage at Food Lion. It will show you I was in Richmond."

They asked a few more questions like how long were Deonte and Nicole involved and if Deonte had life insurance, all to which I didn't know. Their so-called questioning seemed more and more like an interrogation. When I told them I didn't know anything else, one of them handed me his card and said if I remembered anything or if I found out anything to give them a call. I sat on the bench for what seemed like hours even though it had only been a few minutes trying to figure out why someone would kill them. I admit, I wanted to kill both of them when I saw them in bed together and he was getting on my damn nerves but I would never actually do it. Not to mention, I knew I would be the first person they suspected. I was already running from the cops so why would I invite them to come knocking on my door.

My mind quickly shifted to Zeta. How was I going to tell

her that her father was gone and she wouldn't be seeing him again? Then I wondered if she would even understand what I was saying to her. I walked back into the store and headed straight to Larry's office. To be honest, I had mixed feelings about Deonte's death. A part of me was glad the bastard was gone so I didn't have to deal with him anymore but I was sad my little girl was going to have to grow up without her dad. Deonte was a lot of things but he was a good father to Zeta. He was just an asshole of a husband and we were never good together.

When I walked back in the store, Larry had a very weird look on his face. He told me to come to the back because he needed to talk to me. I thought he was going to tell me to take a few days off even though I had just come back. But that wasn't the case at all.

"Zsaset, you know I really like you but this is the second time the cops have come to see you," he said, not even looking me in my face.

"They came to tell me my husband was murdered," I said, tearing up.

"That's what I mean. There is always something dangerous going on around you. I have to protect my customers and this store. So, I'm sorry, but I'm going to have to let you go."

I stood there trying to process what he was saying to me. *Really?* "I'm fired for something I had nothing to do with?" I asked, getting aggressive.

"It doesn't matter. I need you to go. Get your belongings and leave."

Hearing those words made me flip the fuck out. I started knocking over shit, pulling shoes out of the wall and trashing his desk. He was so scared he ran to the front and called security. I grabbed my stuff and as I was leaving I ran my hand along the wall knocking down the shoe displays. When I got to the door, I turned around and said, "Fuck you and this store, Larry."

I was walking to the food court when I spotted two rental cops running to the store. That's when I started to walk even faster. I was in the parking lot, only a few feet away from my car when I noticed a note on my car. When I snatched the note off of my windshield I saw something even more disturbing. My two front tires had been slashed.

"What the fuck?" I said, checking the rest of my car. *This has got to be the month from hell.*

As I was looking at my car, I noticed mall security standing outside the food court surveying the parking lot. I ducked down, slid into my car and started it even though I couldn't go anywhere. While I was waiting for security to go back into the mall, I read the note. **'I want my money by tomorrow bitch. Love Yaya.'** "Are you fucking kidding me? I'm going to kill that bitch!" I yelled, as I slammed my hands down on the steering wheel hurting my already injured arm. Forced to call a cab after I got no answer from neither K-Dog or Dolo, I waited in my car. While I waited, I called triple A to tow my car to the nearest spot for me to get my tires replaced. *What else is going to happen?*

When the Napoleon cab picked me up thirty minutes later, I wanted to go straight home but I had to make a detour to Brenda's house to pick up Zeta. My mind was on overload the whole ride. I was so out of it and tired of having to deal with all the bullshit, I didn't even notice we had been parked outside of Brenda's house for a few minutes. If it wasn't for the cab driver yelling at me that we were there I would probably be still sitting in the car dazed and confused.

Before I knocked on the door, I took a deep breath. I had to put on a happy face for Zeta. When I walked through the door, Zeta was wired as usual. That little girl had a lot of energy. I spoke to Brenda and filled her in on what was going on. She conveyed her condolences and told me that if I needed anything to let her know. The only thing I needed at that moment was a drink.

"Hey, I really hate to bring this up right now but Zeta has been very aggressive to the other kids."

"What do you mean, aggressive?" I asked.

"She's been fighting, using profane language and not listening to me when I ask her not to do something."

"Brenda, I am so sorry. I'm going to talk to her again."

"You know I love Zeta like she's one of my own but I'm sorry, I won't be able to watch her anymore. I have to do what's best for the other kids."

I stared at her for a moment waiting for her to say she was just playing but she didn't. I was pissed off but it wasn't her fault my child didn't know how to act. It was mine. "I totally understand," I said, about to cry.

When we got to the cab, I put her in her booster seat and headed to my apartment. I was so pissed with her and I let it be known on the ride home. I started by telling Zeta how disappointed in her I was. She was probably saying the same thing about me.

"If you keep being a bad girl, I'm going to take all of your toys away."

"Nooooo," she whined.

"Okay, well I need you to stop being a bad girl."

Zeta started frowning. I had to be honest with myself, I was the reason she was acting up. I wasn't the only one going through all of this madness; she was, too.

Overwhelmed and emotionally drained, I hauled our stuff in the house. Zeta was so happy to be back home she went straight up to her room to play with her toys. I poured myself a glass of wine, slipped my sneakers off and plopped on the couch contemplating if I should call Deonte's mom. She hated me and blamed me for the problems in our marriage.

Sitting with a drink in my hand, I dwelled on the culmination of my bad luck and misfortune that had been adding up over the months. I felt like my life was spiraling downward and I was losing all sense of control. I was already feeling down and suicidal. Losing my job was going to put me over the edge. I kept having visions of killing myself and I was running out of justifications not to. I needed help. But who could I turn to?

My self-loathing was interrupted by a loud knock at the door. I damned near spilled my drink. The whistling of the leaves outside had me on edge so I walked over to the door cautiously and looked through the peephole.

What the hell is he doing here? How did he know I was home? I opened the door and hurried him in because the wind was blowing so hard.

"How did you know I was home?" I said, bothered by his presence.

"I'm following you," Dolo said. When I didn't find his comment funny, he laughed at it himself. "I'm just kidding. I went up to the store to apologize for the way I acted earlier. They told me you left early though."

"Oh."

We retreated to the den so I could continue drinking my wine. Moments later, my phone rang. It was Vicki checking on me. I took the call in the living room because I didn't want Zeta to sneak up on me and overhear what happened to her dad.

"I can't believe Larry fired you after the news you got today. What an asshole!" Vicki said, mad as hell.

"I know. He could've just wrote me up. Punk ass bitch!"

"Have you told Zeta yet?" Vicki asked.

"No, she's upstairs playing. I'm just sitting in here with Dolo having a drink."

"Oh, you didn't have to call him to come over. I could've left work early to sit with you."

"I didn't call him over. He said y'all told him I was at home."

"What? No one is here but me. I've been here by myself since you left because one of Larry's kids got sick so he had to leave and I haven't seen Dolo, Zsa!" she said surprised.

She wasn't the only one surprised. *Why did he lie?*

"Okay. Let me call you back," I said.

We hung up and I went straight back in the den to confront him.

"When you went up to the store today, did Larry seem like he was mad I left?"

"Ummm…I didn't see him. Some other chick was there."

"Really, what did she look like?"

"Babe, I don't know. I wasn't really paying her any attention. Why you so touchy today?" he asked.

"There's just a lot of shit going on. I don't know who I can trust and who I can't trust," I said, looking him square in the eyes.

He kissed me and said, "Well, you know you can trust me, right?"

I faked a smile and nodded.

"Truth is, I got some bad news today," I said.

"Oh, what's that," he said, sliding over closer, with added concern.

I laid back on the couch, exhaled and said, "My ex-husband and my friend Nicole are dead."

"Wow, you okay?" he said, with what almost resembled a strange smirk but his eyes read differently. His ass was definitely weird.

"Honestly, I don't know. I mean he's my daughter's father." I was looking down and really wishing Dolo would just leave.

"Oh yeah, and he was tryin' to get back with you."

"He wasn't trying to get back with me."

"Whateva! Do they know who murdered them?"

I turned to him, shocked. "How did you know they were murdered?"

He sat looking at me with this blank stare. "Huh? Ummm…you just said they were," he said with this nervous laugh.

"No! I said they were dead. They could've died in a car crash or in their sleep. Why would you say they were murdered?"

"I don't know. When people die I'm just used to it being because they were murdered." He started to look and feel uncomfortable so he used my being in a bad mood as an excuse to leave. His behavior was getting odder than usual. I would soon find out why his bipolar behavior wasn't so odd after all.

• • •

After Dolo left, I called got a call from Deonte's mother who was understandably distraught. I gave her my condolences and told her that although we had our moments I would never wish any harm to him. I guess she didn't believe me because she cursed me out and told me not to show up to his funeral or she would have me thrown out. I figured it was just the grief talking but then his aunt got on the phone and said if I had hurt Deonte she would see me in hell before I got away with it. His aunt also said she didn't think it was a good idea for Zeta to be there either. She felt she was too young and seeing her father laying in a casket might traumatize her. Well, we at least agreed on that. She was too young.

Deonte's aunt hung up on me so quick I didn't get to ask her if they had caught the person or people responsible. We were still married so I had the right to know that. I knew as the estranged spouse, the first thought people would have is that I did it or I had something to do with it. Which was so ridiculous. If I didn't go to his funeral it would make me look even more guilty.

If I really wanted to be as nasty as they were making me out to be, I could've picked up his body and had him cremated; something I knew his mother was dead set against. But the last thing I needed was another crazy bitch on my hands. But with my new unemployment status and Deonte not around for child support, I was definitely going to fight for the benefits my daughter was entitled to, including his life insurance, if there was a policy. I just needed to wait until they found the killer.

After having another glass of wine, I checked in on my girl's Brina and Sheba. I conferenced them both in so we could all talk. I wanted to see how they were holding up. They were okay and just as curious as I was about who would do something like this.

"Girl, they said it was an execution style killing?" Sheba said.

"Why would someone want them dead? I mean besides

me. They were fucking behind my back if you recall."

"You sure it didn't have anything to do with you?" Brina asked.

Sheba and I both said, "What?" at the same time.

"Think about it. Someone tried to kill you, they actually killed Quan, you keep having weird shit happen and some crazy guy is following you." Brina said.

"Zsa, she might be right."

"Oh God. I didn't even think about that," I said. She gave me something to think about. *What if this did have something to do with me?* "I have to find out what's going on."

Our conspiracy theories went on for about an hour. After I hung up the phone, Zeta came walking down the stairs.

"Mommy, I want to call my daddy," she said.

Tears fell from my eyes. I tried to wipe them away before she saw me. "Sweetie, come here for a moment."

"No mommy, I want to call daddy now," she said, grabbing my cell phone.

"Zeta, come here I need to talk to you," I said raising my voice.

Her head hung low as she walked over to me slowly. I picked her up and sat her on the couch next to me. 'Okay let's see. Remember when we put your fish Barbie in that cute little box and we put it in the ground behind the house?"

"Yes, you said Barbie went to live with God in heaven."

"Right! Well, God needed another angel so he bought your daddy up to heaven to be with Barbie."

"When is he coming back?"

I eased closer to her and kissed her on her forehead. "He's not coming back, baby. He's going to live in heaven for good but he'll always be right here in your heart," I said pointing. "And he's always going to be looking down from heaven to protect you, okay?"

A look of despair was on her face. I still wasn't sure if she fully understood or if she thought this was something that was temporary. The only thing I could do at that moment was hold her and let her know she still had me. For whatever that was. I barely had myself.

...SIX...

The next day when my car was ready to be picked up, I asked Vicki to give me ride to the tire shop. When the guy told me I owed two hundred and eighty dollars, I started to leave the bitch there. I could barely pay the note, I didn't even figure in how much the maintenance would cost to keep it up. I paid the guy and walked out with my pockets feeling a whole lot lighter. I went over to Vicki's car to get Zeta so we could go home but she had already talked Vicki into taking her with her to the mall.

"Vicki, you don't have to do that. You've kept her so much already."

"Girl, I love keeping my baby. She's such a good girl."

"Who? Not this crazy girl right her," I said, rubbing Zeta cheeks. She got so tickled when I did that.

I gave her a kiss and handed her twenty dollars so she could buy a toy. Seeing her eyes light up in spite of just finding out she wouldn't be seeing her father again was reassuring that she was going to be okay. When Vicki turned the car on and started pulling off, Zeta waved good-bye to me. I got into my car and headed home. I was almost home when Dolo called. *What the hell does he want?* I thought. I was getting so sick of his bullshit and crazy behavior. I had enough craziness going on in my life and he was adding to it.

"Hello."

"What up ma?"

I rolled my eyes so hard they almost rolled out of my

head. "Nothing."

"Whatchu doin'?"

I took a deep breath. "I just picked my car up from the shop."

"How much did they charge you?"

"Three eighty," I said inflating the price.

"Aight, I'll give it back to you when I see you."

"Okay," I said really dry.

"I gotta go take care of somethin' so I'll hit you up later. Love you."

I looked at my phone like maybe the lines got crossed or something. *I know this nigga ain't telling me he loves me after the way he's been acting.* He stayed on the line like he was waiting for me to say it back but I hit him with an "Okay, talk to you later."

Ten minutes later, I pulled into a parking spot in front of my apartment, looked in my rearview mirror, and saw a car pull behind me. When I got out my car and saw who it was, my blood began to boil immediately. We locked eyes for a moment then she got out of the car.

"Hey Zsa! I see you got them tires fixed, girl. Oh and this ain't no patch job, these some new joints," she said, inspecting my tires.

"I wouldn't need new tires if it wasn't for your stupid, ignorant ass."

"Allll shit! So I'm ignorant?" she asked, swinging her 26-inch, two-toned Brazilian weave.

"And stupid...don't forget stupid," I said, ready to take her damn head off.

"Bitch, you always talkin' shit like you betta than me."

"That's because I am."

She got up in my face. "Is that so? You runnin' round here killin' mothafuckas... goin' from one drug dealer to the next and you think you betta than me." She got even closer because I had moved back a little. "You aint nothin' but a trashy ho dressed in designer clothes. And just like they took yo' son they gonna take yo' daughter cause you ain't shit bitch!"

Next thing I knew we were scrapping like Mayweather and Pacquiao. Yaya had an advantage over me. She was bigger and my arm had still not fully recovered but I was hanging in there with her ass. I had to let her know I wasn't scared of her. We were kicking and punching each other wildly.

"Bitch, you gon respect me!" she yelled, as we fell to the ground screaming and pulling each other's hair.

I got the upper hand when I was able to get up off the ground before her slow ratchet ass could. My arm was throbbing so I started stomping her.

"No, bitch you're going to respect me!"

She grabbed one of my legs and pulled me down again. We were rolling around in the grass when I heard someone say 'you get Yaya'. It was K-Dog and Coley. They were trying to break us up but we wouldn't let go of each other's hair.

"Y'all stop!" K-Dog yelled.

"Tell that bitch to let go of my hair," I screamed.

"You let go of my damn hair," Yaya yelled back.

Stubborn, we both laid on the ground refusing to let go.

"Okay, fuck it. Both y'all asses goin' to jail if the police come," K-Dog shouted.

The last thing I needed was to go to jail when I was trying to show Mrs. Smith that I was responsible enough to get Ryan back so I let her go after one last hard yank. She let me go after she hit me one last time. We both got up out of breath and dirty.

"Stupid bitch!" I yelled, as I tried to get the grass out of my hair.

"I got yo' stupid bitch," she yelled and lunged toward me.

Coley quickly grabbed Yaya as K-Dog pushed me in the house.

I was brushing the dirt out of my hair and readjusting my ripped shirt when K-Dog walked back outside. He returned a few minutes later.

"What the hell happened?" he asked.

"That crazy bitch came over then she started running her damn mouth and the next thing I know we were fighting."

"O.B gotta do somethin' bout her!"

"A'ight, she's gone," Coley said busting in the door.

"I'll be back in a few," I said pissed.

I was so furious, I stomped up the stairs to take a shower. I got out of my grass stained clothes and went into my bathroom. My hands shook as I stood in the mirror and inspected my face for scratches. I had a few so I put some antiseptic rinse on them. I then inspected my body. I had a few bruises and my arm looked swollen.

When I stepped into the shower the hot water running down my body felt so good. I put some shampoo in my hand and worked into my scalp. After I was sure the dirt and grass was out, I put some deep conditioner on it and let it sit for ten minutes. I then lathered up my shower sponge and cleaned my body of grass and dirt that was on my skin. Then it dawned on me that Yaya could be mad enough to just forget all about the money and let Detective Berry come and arrest me. *Why didn't I just ignore her and come in the house? Well what's done is done now,* I thought.

After I was clean, I put on some yoga pants and a t-shirt. I let my hair air dry because there was no way I could lift my arms to do it. My body was hurting so bad I had to take a Percocet. I looked in the bottle and saw I was almost out so I needed to make sure I called my doctor to get a refill. Life without those pills would probably be unbearable.

I was walking down the stairs when I heard K-Dog and Coley having a serious conversation.

"God, if you want me to I can just do Yaya the same way I did Lina," Coley said.

"I been so busy I forgot to ask you. How did you handle that snitchin' bitch?"

"I had her meet me in Petersburg. I told her I knew she snitched so now we just needed to talk to you face to face and out of Richmond about what our next move is."

"She fell for that?"

"Not at first. She played dumb but I told her it was okay and that I understood how detectives play mind games with you. When she arrived I told her that we were both marked and that her damn sister was blackmailin' O.B and Zsaset. I told her Yaya told us she snitched. That was the only way I could make sure she wouldn't call Yaya while we were together. Then we drove to Atlanta and checked into a hotel. I got her drunk, fucked her then when she fell asleep I stuck her with a needle full of Xanax and heroin. I left her at that hotel, checked into another hotel then drove back here the next day."

Remind me never to get him mad, I thought to myself as I held my chest.

"You sure they can't trace it back to you?" K-Dog asked.

"Naw, I wore a disguise and I borrowed someone's car so I didn't have to drive mine."

"How you know she's dead?"

"The morning news said they found a woman dead at the hotel we stayed at so they must've found her."

"That's what's up. I have to be careful with Yaya though cause she workin' with that detective."

"We'll just have to get rid of his ass too."

"Naw, that'll bring too much heat. Don't worry, I'll get her ass. I'm tired of her fuckin' wit Zsa."

"You really care bout' her, don't you?"

K-Dog was slow to respond then he said, "What's takin' her so long?"

I walked down the rest of the stairs and poured myself a glass of wine.

"Zsa, I promise you we will deal with Yaya," K-Dog said. "Just stay away from her and don't keep lettin' her get to you."

"Okay," I said, taking a seat. "Where's O.B?"

"He's at the new trap house in Mosby," Coley said.

"Let's hope he doesn't get robbed again," K-Dog said

sarcastically.

"So, has this ever happened before?" I asked.

"Yeah like twice in Mosby not including the time you were there. This is our fourth spot," K-Dog said.

"It happened in Mosby a couple months before you got here. He had some chick holding his piece that time, too. What good is it if somebody else got it? You know ain't no chick gonna blaze." Coley looked at me. "Well, you did but the other dumb chicks ain't know what to do."

He gave me his gun that night too, I thought to myself.

"I don't know what's goin' on with him but he betta get his shit together cause I can't keep takin' these L's," K-Dog said sternly.

We talked a few more minutes, then K-Dog and Coley left. I continued to sit on the couch and sip on my wine. My mind was working overtime. I wondered why he didn't answer Coley's question. If he didn't care about me in a romantic way, he would've just said no. He didn't do that. He skipped the question completely leaving me to wonder if what Brina said was true.

54

...SEVEN...

While Zeta played in her room, I sat on the edge of my bed drinking wine straight out of the bottle drowning in my sorrows. It was too early to be drinking but I had to find some way to soothe my pain. Ryan was placed in foster care permanently, Deonte and Nicole were dead and I still couldn't believe I had been shot and Quan had been killed. There was so much stuff going through my head. It was all too much. *Who could've killed them? And why didn't Ryan want to come live with me? More importantly, who shot me and killed Quan?* As I sat puzzled, my already horrible day was about to get worse.

Once I emptied the bottle, I headed downstairs to grab another bottle of wine from the kitchen. Halfway down the stairs, there was a knock at the door. I looked through the peephole and was surprised to see that it was K-dog. I took a deep breath before I opened the door.

"Hey," I said, trying not to slur.

"Hey Z, sorry to drop by unannounced but I've got some bad news for you."

"Dog, I really can't take any more. I'm already drunk and it's not even...what time is it anyway?"

"It's almost five."

"I've been drinking since like one, pretty much as soon as I got up today," I said, taking a seat at the kitchen table.

"Well, I hope you can sober up to hear this shit I got to

tell you."

"It can't wait? You really gonna tell me anyway?"

"Listen Zsa, we were right about Dolo."

"What? What do you mean?"

"It was Dolo and his crew that shot you and killed Quan."

I couldn't believe my ears. I knew Dolo was capable of some unthinkable shit but I couldn't understand what his reason would've been to shoot me and take Quan out.

"Are you sure?" I asked, knowing he was sure. I just wanted him not to be this time.

"C'mon now, I only speak the truth. You know me better than that. I'm positive. These streets talk more than Miss Benita," he said referencing the old classic TV show 'In Living Color'.

"Oh my Godddddd!" I said in disbelief. My jaw dropped and I was just speechless. All I could do was cover my face and sob. *How incredibly stupid of me? I was sleeping with the man who shot me and killed my friend. He probably got a good laugh out of making a fool of me.* Fury exploded inside me. If he were standing in front of me at that moment I probably would've shot him with the very gun he gave me.

"Why would he do something like this?" I said, my voice quivering.

"Zsaset, we didn't tell you this but when we first got to Richmond we moved in on Dolo's turf. We took over a couple of his areas and our product was better so we took a lot of his customers. He got pissed. He hit one our guy's…we hit one of his," K-Dog explained

"Why are you just telling me this?"

"We thought the beef was over but apparently he doesn't feel that way."

"Now what's going to happen?"

"I told Quan's dad so shit is about to get real round here. Don't go near that dude. Don't even talk to him on the phone. Trust me, you don't want to be in the middle of this shit."

"Okay," I said, with a mixture of emotions. A part of me wanted to confront Dolo but the other part didn't want to ever see his face again. I could feel rage going through my veins. I wanted to rip Dolo limb to limb with my hands.

K-Dog got up to leave. I walked to him to the door, exasperated.

"Just be careful, baby girl," he said, sliding his arms around me to give me a hug.

I told him I would and closed the door. When I turned around Cindy was creeping back to her room. *Was this bitch listening to our conversation?* I walked to her room and asked her what she was doing that night. She told me she was about to jump into the shower because she was going out.

"Okay, well have fun. I'm going to take a nap," I said being nice but inside I was ready to roar.

I waited until she got into the shower then I snuck into her room. I looked around for her cell phone but I couldn't find it. I kept listening as the water ran to make sure Cindy didn't catch me snooping through her stuff. All of sudden, I heard her Samsung Galaxy begin to vibrate. I listened as the sound guided me to her bed. I pulled her covers back and grabbed the phone. *This bitch ain't even smart enough to lock her damn phone,* I thought shaking my head. There were several text messages but the one that stuck out the most from the one from a familiar number. I didn't need to open it because it displayed the first two lines. **Hey, I got your message. You sure?** The water stopped, so I slid the phone back under her covers and tip toed out of her room. When I got back to my room, I fell to the floor. I felt like I had been punched in the gut. I didn't know which was worse. Finding out Dolo shot me or knowing that Cindy was stabbing me in the back this whole time. It was all coming together for me now. *Why she wanted to be my roommate, why she was asking so many questions and how he knew almost everything I did.* An ass kicking was too good for her. She needed to be dealt with on a permanent level and I knew just the person to do it.

Reaching for my phone, I dialed K-Dog.

"Hey Z, what's up?"

"You're not going to believe what I just found out," I said, stressed.

"What happened?" he asked nervous.

I told him about the text and who the text was from. I could hear Cindy talking while I was on the phone with K-Dog so I told him to hold on for a second. I crept over to her door. She wasn't talking loud enough for me to everything she said but I did hear enough. I slipped down the stairs and then told K-Dog I was back.

"She's on her way to meet him now."

"Okay, keep her there. We're at the gas station down the street. We'll be there in fifteen minutes."

"Alright."

I sat on the couch with a glass of wine praying she didn't leave before they arrived. Five minutes later, she came bouncing down the stairs. I prepared to put on my Oscar award performance. When Cindy saw me on the couch crying, she ran over and asked me what was wrong. I reached out my arms. She sat down next to me and hugged me. I then laid my head in her lap. As I was talking, she was texting. No doubt, letting him know she was running late.

"I'm so stressed out. I just feel like I'm a failure," I said, in between crying.

"You're not a failure. We all go through rough patches," she said, preoccupied.

I sat up and wiped my face. "I don't even know who I can trust anymore." I took my hand and ran it down the side of her face. "Thank God I have you in my life. I know you would never betray me."

"Of course not. You're like a sister to me."

Oh this bitch is good....but I'm better.

"Look, let me make this quick run, I'll come back and we can watch movies for the rest of the night."

When Zeta came down the stairs, I wiped my face so she

wouldn't think something was wrong for real.

"Can you stay a few minutes more?"

"No, I'm already late but I'll be right back."

"Can I go, Cindy?" Zeta asked, grabbing her arm.

"Not this time munchkin, but I'll be back."

She jumped up, grabbed her bag and went out the door. I grabbed my keys, scooped up my phone and quickly called K-Dog. I peeped out of the window to make sure she was gone then pulled Zeta by the arm out the door.

"She just left!" I said, running to my car.

"We're right around the corner so we'll see her when she comes out of the complex."

I was about to let him know I was going to follow her when he cut me off. "I see her. I gotta go."

I didn't even secure Zeta in the seat belt, I just peeled off.

I Shoulda' SEEN HIM Coming 2

...EIGHT...

Driving down Hull Street, I watched from several cars back as K-Dog tried to catch up to Cindy in his hooptie without speeding. He always had a gun on him, so I guess he was making sure he didn't get pulled over. For a mile, we all followed her until she was on a street that was barely lit. That's when K-Dog made his move. He tapped her bumper. Not hard enough to do damage but enough to get her to stop and assess the damage. As soon as her feet hit the pavement, Coley and O.B hopped out and confronted her. I pulled up behind them. As soon as they spotted my car, K-Dog called my phone and lit into me.

"Look, that bitch betrayed me and I'm going to find out why. So what's the plan?"

"Just follow us!" he said, mad as hell.

O.B was so livid he yanked her by her blond tresses and pushed her towards K-Dog's car. Walking closely behind her, O.B walked her to the back seat of the car. Coley, wearing black gloves, got into Cindy's car. K-Dog pulled out and Coley followed then I followed Coley. K-Dog drove to a wooded area near the western end of Henrico County and pulled up on the gravel of a secluded area. I hit the ignition to cut the car off and then looked at my daughter. *This is why she acts the way she does. I always have her around my madness.*

Before I got out, I started a cartoon on my car's DVD player and told Zeta to watch it until I came back. I turned the

61

volume up really loud so Zeta couldn't hear what was going on. Amped up, I got out of my car and into K-Dog's then gave that bitch the stare down from hell. She pretended not to know what was going on. But when O.B. smacked her with the butt of the gun and told her we knew who she was working for, she started crying hysterically. We ignored her as she begged and pleaded with us to let her go.

"Look, it wasn't my idea. I didn't want to go along with it but he said if I didn't he would kill my mother."

"When did he first approach you?" Cindy turned her head away in shame. "When?" O.B yelled.

Cindy jumped. "It was when he found out Zsaset worked in Lady Foot Locker. He went in there to spy on her and overheard her and Vicki talking about her needing a roommate. I was already working at McDonald's. He saw her eating McDonalds one day and figured that's how he could get close to her…to get close to y'all."

I hopped across the seat and punched her ass so hard her eyes rolled back. "Bitch, I should've known your trashy ass won't shit!" I continued to punch and pull her hair until K-Dog pulled me off of her.

"Stop, we need to talk to her. I need to know everythin' this mothafucka is up to," K-Dog yelled.

Out of breath and half out my mind, I pushed my hair out of my face. Then I turned around in my seat and pouted like a spoiled brat. "Hurry up cause I'm not finished with that bitch," I yelled, shaking my leg.

"So, we were right. He did kill Quan and shoot Zsa," O.B said, smacking her in the face.

She grabbed her face and let out a screech. "Yes," she said, nodding her head.

"I shoulda known that Dolo wasn't over our beef," K-Dog said frustrated.

"So, you were gonna stand by and help this nigga kill all of us? Did you even think about Zeta? Or my child, for that matter?" O.B asked, dealing a blow to her head.

Cindy looked out the window hoping for any sign of help but there was none. She kept reciting the Lord's Prayer which infuriated me even more.

"Bitch, shut the fuck up! It's too late to be calling on God," I yelled.

K-Dog ordered O.B to get Cindy out. Parked next to us, Coley exited Cindy's car. They all stood at the back of Cindy's car as I checked on Zeta.

"Who's in the car?" K-Dog asked.

"Zeta, she's okay."

"Why the hell would you bring her with you? I told you to let me handle this," he yelled.

"She's watching a cartoon. She's fine. Can we get back to the real problem?"

K-Dog looked at Cindy and said to her, "Give me a reason to let you live."

O.B and Coley stood confused. "God, we not lettin' this bitch go! As far as I'm concerned she killed Quan, too," O.B said. He then spit on her.

"If you want to live you need to start talkin'? What is he plannin' next? What else has he done we don't know about? Start talkin'," K-Dog yelled.

"I swear to you I don't know," she cried. "I just know he did something to make sure Zsaset stayed with him. He didn't tell me what though I swear."

"He did something to make me stay with him," I repeated. "What did he do?"

"I don't know. He left town one night and said after that night he wouldn't have to worry about you ever leaving him."

Tired of the riddles, K-Dog instructed Coley to open up Cindy's trunk. He then walked to his trunk and pulled out a gas can. Cindy knew her fate was sealed unless she did something so she tried to make a run for it. She didn't get far because O.B shot her in the leg.

"Son, what the fuck are you doin'? Zeta's in the car?" K-Dog asked.

O.B was so pissed off he told K-Dog to shut up as he dragged her back to the car and dumped her in the trunk. It was getting out of control so K-Dog told me to leave but I wanted to see that bitch die.

"Get the hell out of here!" he yelled.

I walked to my car as he quickly doused her with gasoline. He then poured gasoline from the car in a line away from them and lit the spot with a match. You could hear Cindy's muffled screams as she kicked and pounded inside the trunk as I was sitting down in my car. I started my car, put in gear and pulled off. I looked in my rear view mirror and saw the fire quickly moved towards Cindy's Toyota Camry as all three men jumped in K-Dog's car and sped off. The sky lit up as her car was engulfed in flames.

As we were driving back to the Southside of Richmond, K-Dog called me. I knew he was angry so I didn't answer it. He caught up with me at a light and held his phone to his ear. *Shit!* I thought.

He called again. This time I answered. "What?"

"Go back to your place and get rid of all of her shit. You know this is goin' to make the news tomorrow, right?"

"No, it won't. Tomorrow is Sept 11th and the world will be too busy reflecting on that. She'll be a footnote in the paper and that's about it," I said confident then hung up.

Cindy played a dangerous game and in the end she lost.

● ● ●

As soon as Zeta and I got inside the house, I went straight to the bottle of Vodka that was on the kitchen counter. I poured myself a drink and sat down. I still couldn't process the fact that Cindy and Dolo were playing me the whole time. At this point, he was the enemy and I should have been smarter.

A few hours had passed by and I didn't realize I fell asleep out on the couch. I was awakened by a loud knock at the door. At the same time, my phone started to vibrate. I looked at the phone and the screen read 'Dolo'. I didn't want to talk to him so I ignored his call. Zeta was almost four now and she was picking up on every little thing I said and did. She would've definitely heard some bad words and would've been upset seeing her mother go postal on Dolo's ass.

The knock at the door continued, so I looked out the window to see who it was as Dolo continued to call my phone again.

"Got damn. Calling my phone and banging on the door. What the fuck is wrong with this nigga?" I whispered.

Pissed that I wouldn't answer the door, he started pounding so hard my pictures almost fell off the wall.

My phone vibrated again.

Why is he fucking serial calling me?

The knocking at the door continued louder and harder. I was so terrified, I couldn't move.

"I know what you did and I know all about Cindy so go away or I'm going to call the police," I said from the other side of the door.

"What you talkin' bout?

"Drop the act! I know it was you that shot me and killed my brother."

"It wasn't me. It was my boys!" he yelled.

I could hear him breathing heavily. Then he started banging on my windows. *WTF is he doing? What a psycho! Does he really think beating on my door and windows is going to make me let him in?*

"I called the police! They're on their way!" I yelled.

His knocking was so loud, I thought it was gunshots. He kept hollering, "Open the door! Open the damn door Zsaset!"

I got on my knees and crawled to kitchen to retrieve a knife. Then I pushed my coffee table in front of the door. I knew if he got in he would kill me but not without a fight.

After a few minutes, the knocking stopped but I knew it wasn't over. Dolo hated rejection and he wasn't going to simply walk away.

"That's cool. I'll check on you tomorrow," he said.

Seriously, who does this bullshit! Is he really this crazy? I thought as I wiped the tears that had fallen down my face. "I'll leave now but just know that it's not over until I say it's over," he said. He started to walk away but then came back. "You can't get rid of me that easily." Dolo's demeanor and attitude changed. He stood outside my window ranting and raving. "Do you know what I did to make this shit happen for us? You think it was just fate? I put a lot into makin' sure you and I were together and you think I'm just goin' to let you go just like that? Think again, Ma, cause the best is yet to come," he said before finally leaving.

I thought he was just talking shit but I found out real soon that wasn't the case. I said before that he was crazy and he proved to me that I was right. He wasn't just crazy he was a sociopath.

What in the world had I gotten myself into? Maybe I should have returned to Norfolk as K-Dog suggested. Everything, and I do mean everything, was spiraling out of control.

...NINE...

I think K-Dog was feeling guilty. He hadn't been over in a while so he decided to stop by and play cards with me one Friday evening. I was in such a bad way, and I wasn't taking care of myself. My hair was all over my head and my fingernails hadn't been done in months. I had no reason to get cute. Unfortunately, I had lost my job so my days and nights were spent in the house and I wasn't seeing Dolo anymore. Of course, he refused to accept it. He would call all day and night but I wouldn't answer. When that didn't work he would pop up at my apartment off and on just to make sure I didn't have someone else over. I felt like a prisoner in my own apartment. I couldn't sleep because he would show up in the middle of the night sometimes banging on my damn door. As soon as my lease was up, I was definitely moving somewhere else.

As much as I complained about how fucked up my life was, I was lucky to still be in my place. If it wasn't for K-Dog and O.B paying my bills, I would've had to move back to their place. O.B even managed to give Yaya some money to keep her off my back for a minute. Plus, he still had to give her money to keep his secret. She still wouldn't tell him where his son was though and every lead he had about his son turned out to be a dead end. Poor guy was going through it with that chick. The money shut her up for a minute but I knew it was only a matter of time before she would be back for more. My guess is she was

67

too busy looking for her missing sister Lina.

When I went to offer him a beer I saw that I was out, so I put Zeta's jacket on and we all rode up to the store. As we were driving, Ryan came to mind. I pulled out my phone and called the foster home where he was staying.

"Hello," a man answered in a whisper.

"Hi this is Zsaset Jones. I was wondering if I could speak to my son, Ryan."

"Miss Jones, I'm afraid that won't be possible."

"Why? What happened?" I asked frantic.

"The children are asleep. We have a strict eight thirty lights out policy. You'll have to call back tomorrow."

"Okay," I said aggravated.

I tried to regain my composure. He scared the hell out of me then he tells me they have an eight thirty bedtime. I was getting so sick of being told what I can and can't do with my child. I hung the phone and began to rant and rave to K-Dog.

"This shit is so ridiculous!"

"He'll be back with you soon then you won't have to deal with their bullshit anymore," K-Dog said trying to cheer me up.

As soon as we stepped out of the car, I noticed that same guy standing in front of the store. He looked straight at me and started smiling. I'd had enough of him.

"That's the guy I was telling you about. The one who's been following me," I said to K-Dog. Before K-Dog could utter a word, I ran up on the guy. "Why are you following me?" I asked. "Did Dolo hire you?"

"I have no idea what you're talkin' about," the guy said with a sinful grin.

K-Dog looked at me like I was losing my mind but I wasn't. This guy was really following me and I didn't know why.

"K-Dog, I've seen this guy like three or four times and he's always staring at me with this look."

"Look, maybe it's just a coincidence." He went on. "It's

not a crime for people to stare at you, Zsaset. Let me handle this," he whispered, as he handed me a hundred dollar bill. "Go, get what you need. I'll be there in a sec."

Was it possible that this was all in my head? Even I was starting to doubt myself. I was willing to let it go for now but if I saw this dude again I was going to find out who he was.

K-Dog decided to talk to the guy to see if he could get any information out of him. I grabbed Zeta out of her car seat and went into the store and grabbed a six pack of beers and some chips.

"Mommy, mommy can I have some candy?"

"No, you have candy at home," I told Zeta.

She completely lost it. She fell on the ground and started rolling around on the floor. I snatched her little ass up and drug her to the counter kicking and screaming. By the time K-Dog walked in, I was already at the counter paying for my beer.

"What did the guy say? Why is he following me?" I asked anxiously.

"He said he doesn't know what you're talkin' bout and he thinks you're followin' him?"

"He's such a liar!" I bolted toward the door but he grabbed me. "Will you stop? Forget him." I stood there tapping my foot on the ground. I wanted to go punch that mothafucka right in the face. I could barely hear what K-Dog was saying so I shook Zeta real hard and told her to shut up. Then I turned my attention back to K-Dog.

"Whoa, what's wrong with her?" K-Dog asked because Zeta was still crying.

"She wants some candy, but she has some at home."

K-Dog walked to the candy aisle, grabbed a pack of M&M's with peanuts and gave them to her. He told the guy to add them to the beer.

"I told her she couldn't have any," I said, looking at him angrily.

"I know, but I don't like to see her cry. Just like I don't like to see you cry."

I turned my head back to the cashier. I felt so awkward. I handed the guy the money and waited for the change. When I tried to give the change to K-Dog he told me to keep it. I thanked him and headed to the door to leave the store. *Maybe Brina was right. Maybe K-Dog does have feelings for me.*

Fed up with this dude, I tapped the camera icon on my phone and started snapping pictures of him. He tried hiding behind a pole but I already had a good shot of him. "Zsaset, what are you doing?" K-Dog asked pissed.

"Taking a picture of his ass," I said snapping back.

"Let me get you home before you really make a scene out here."

As we pulled out of the parking lot, the guy eyed us until we were out of sight with this sneaky look in his eyes. I had a sick feeling that it wouldn't be long before the guy's identity would be revealed to me. I just didn't know it would be so soon.

●●●

The moment we were back at my place, I turned on my iPad and put on a cartoon for Zeta. Once she was straight, I cracked open a beer, sat down at the table and started shuffling the cards.

"You ready to get your butt beat again?"

"Yeah whatever," K-dog yelled, as he slammed his stack of money on the table.

I had just started shuffling the cards when K-Dog's phone rang.

"What up?" he yelled into the receiver.

While he talked, I dealt the cards. "Alright, I'll ask her," he said, then hung up.

"What's going on?" I asked.

"Coley wants to know if you want him to come stay here a couple of days?"

"Why?"

"Just in case Dolo comes back or gets upset."

"Upset about what? Cindy?" I asked concerned.

"Yeah. I mean we don't really know how close they were."

I took out two cigarettes. I lit one for myself and handed the other one to K-Dog.

"So, what's Coley like? I've never really talked to him," I asked.

"He's good people and you don't have to worry about him bringin' any drama to your crib. And he'll give you somethin' on the rent if you let him stay here permanently. I know he gotta be tired of stayin' in hotels. I would let him stay with us but we gotta couple of guys there right now. I gotta get this gold stacked back up so I bought a few niggas back from NY with me."

"That's fine. I need the money and I would actually feel a little safer with a man in the house."

"Cool. I'ma text him."

It only took Coley fifteen minutes to get to my place. When he walked in, I had never noticed what a cutie Coley was until that night. He was a dark-skinned, shorty with a slim build. His sexy light brown eyes gave him that extra umph. I couldn't keep my eyes off the ice that dripped from his neck. I guess since he got rid of that dead weight, that they called Lina, things were starting to look up for him. I was a little skeptical about his loyalty but since he kept his mouth closed about the shooting and K-Dog was still dealing with him, I left it alone.

"What up God?" K-Dog asked, Coley letting him in.

"Yo son, who all them lil niggas at the rest?"

K-Dog started laughing. "I knew you were gonna ask me that."

"Yo, I couldn't find a beer in that piece. Niggas done drank up everythin'."

K-Dog couldn't stop laughing, so Coley looked at me for an explanation. All I could do was shrug my shoulders because I didn't know any of them.

"That's them lil niggas from Brownsville. When we link up with them people tomorrow I'ma put them dudes to work."

"Where O.B?" Coley asked.

"He in Jackson Ward finding a new spot for us out there, nah mean. Shit bout to be back to normal."

"Okay, that's what's up."

"Zsaset, I gotta make a quick run. Do you need anythin' while I'm out?" K-Dog said, as he got up grabbing his jacket from the back of the chair.

"No, I'm good." I said.

"A'ight. I'll be right back."

I figured while K-Dog was gone, I would try to get to know Coley a little better. The only time we had ever really had a conversation is when we were talking about Lina and Yaya. Other than that, I didn't know too much about him. I kept asking him questions hoping he would open up a little. A few minutes later, there was a horn blowing loudly outside. I looked out the window and saw that it was K-Dog. Coley's phone rang right after.

"K-Dog told me to come outside. He needs to talk to me."

I followed to be nosy. I ended up talking and laughing for about an hour with them outside. We talked about the fist fight I had with O.B to Yaya's Miralax mishap. It was like old times for a minute. Then they started to talk about getting rid of Yaya's ass. I was all for that conversation.

"The only reason I haven't done it yet is because I don't know if that Detective guy has a tail on her."

"Then they'll just have to get wet up, too," Coley said with a wild eyed look.

"Son, killing some cops is going to bring us a whole new set of problems we don't need. Don't worry, I'ma get that bitch."

"God, that needs to happen quick. She's too much of a liability," Coley said.

"Yes, so I can have some damn peace," I added.

"You and O.B both. That bitch got that nigga so fucked up, he's lost like ten pounds," K-Dog said laughing.

Getting tired, I gave K-Dog and hug. "Alright crazy, I'm going in the house." I said.

"Word, I got to go, too. Coley man, I'll pick you up tomorrow," K-Dog said, opening up his car door and taking a seat.

"Alright, Dog. What time we doin' that thang?"

"As soon as my man calls."

"What thing," I asked out of curiosity.

"None ya," K-Dog said.

He didn't have to tell me but I knew it had to do with his new contact since Quan's dad had cut him off.

"Ha Ha," I smirked, as I walked away. Coley followed. As I was walking up the sidewalk, I noticed that all of my neighbor's lights were off. I looked back at the parking lot and his car was gone. *That's strange for him to not be home at this time. He must be still at work,* I thought.

I got to my door and saw it was slightly open. I was alarmed at first but then I figured maybe I didn't close it all the way shut. Coley and I walked in and locked up for the night. I immediately went upstairs to check on Zeta.

She was still asleep in her room so I looked in Cindy's room and it was so messy I could barely get in there. She had shit everywhere.

I went back down stairs and asked Coley if he mind sleeping on the couch because Cindy had stuff on her bed. I promised him I would clean it up the next morning

"No. That's cool," he said.

"Okay," I said. I then handed him some blankets.

I was incredibly tired and anxious to get in bed. I turned down my bed sheets, took off my clothes and went into the bathroom to take a shower. After finishing, I came back into the room and was surprised to find that it was dark and only slightly lit by the street lights, because I was sure I had left the light on. I hesitated for just a moment and then figured Zeta must have come in and got in my bed. Actually, I could hear her breathing in the bed. I groped my way over to the bed and sat down to put some Vitamin E on the scar from my shoulder surgery.

"Good night, Zeta Beta," I said. She didn't respond.

As I slid one leg between the sheets, I felt an adult body in my bed. Then I heard a voice say, "Bitch, I told you, you were gonna pay." My heart pounded.

"Oh my God! What the hell are you doing in my house? Get out," I screamed, as I jumped out of bed and ran. I didn't get far because I tripped over my shoe. When he grabbed me by the hair, he asked if I knew who he was through gritted teeth. I drew a blank because his face was covered by a ski mask. When he pulled it off, I knew exactly who he was. Without hesitation, I started yelling at the top of my lungs. Coley came running upstairs with his gun to my defense. By this time, the guy was holding a gun to my head.

"Gimme yo' gun," he said.

"Look, son, don't hurt her. What you want...money...huh? I have plenty of money downstairs. Just let her go and we can go and get it."

The guy, offended by Coley's offer, cocked the gun and sneered.

"This ain't 'bout no money, nigga. It's about this bitch right here gettin' what she deserves."

"Okay, just calm down. What's your name?" Coley asked, handing the guy his gun.

"My name is Ra, Rashaad," he said in a rough tone

"Okay Ra, look we're both God bodies." Coley pulled up his sleeve to show him his tattoo that read the name 'Supreme.' "Let's just talk about this."

"Fuck…talkin'…God," he said with emphasis.

Coley started talking to him, and automatically knew that Ra was a Five Percenter because of his name. He hoped to get him to think rational thoughts. But it backfired. In a rage, he dragged me back into my room and yanked the phone cord out of the wall. With the gun pointed to my head, he shoved us both down the stairs.

The situation was so surreal. I was helpless. Here we were sitting in my dining room with a gun pointed at us. It was the guy with the scar that I suspected of following me. This man was completely out of control. His eyes were blood shot and he was shaking like a tree in the middle of a storm. I couldn't grasp what was happening.

But reality set back in when he started preaching. "At last, you're gonna feel the pain I felt when you shot my 'lil brother and left him there to die."

"Look, there must be some kind of mistake. I don't even know who your brother is."

"Of course you do, bitch! One of the guys you killed in Mosby Court was my brother. Then to top it all off y'all didn't get arrested because Coley, you, confessed and said you were the shooter and you were being robbed. It was your house so no charges were filed. Y'all planted that dirty gun on him and made it seem like y'all shot him with his own gun. That's some dirty shit."

Coley and I looked at each other, surprised that Ra knew everything that happened. *How could he though?* We were the only ones in the apartment.

"I'm sorry but he was trying to rob and kill us. I don't know who shot him."

"Bitch, it was you who shot him."

This shit wasn't adding up. The only people in the house that knew what happened were me, O.B, Lina and Coley. Then again, Lina told Yaya who was working with Detective Berry. Ra got up and turned on my Bluetooth speaker. He found a radio station then turned the volume up as high as it would go. Between my neighbors not being home and the music up so high, I doubted if anyone would come help us.

Coley and I were forced to sit down on the sofa and remain quiet as Ra tore through the house like a deranged animal. I didn't have proof, but I was sure he was on drugs. Out of breath, he sat at the table drinking Gin straight from the bottle. No, this nigga ain't drinking up all my shit. That was a brand new bottle. Mixing the drugs and the gin made him even crazier. We were fucked.

Scared for our lives, Coley and I sat motionless for an hour listening to him read scriptures from the Bible. *Ain't this a bitch?* He's trying to school us on the Lord. Fed up with his psycho game, I jumped up. "You need to understand that your brother was trying to kill me and my friends. I was just protecting myself." I screamed.

"They weren't gonna kill anybody. They were just gonna take the dope and the money like they were told to do."

"Told by who?" Coley and I said unison.

Agitated by our question, he pulled out his gun and held it to my throat. "I'm only gonna tell you one more time. I want you to sit your ass down and shut the fuck up."

My knees weakened when I heard the tone in his voice. I was a lot of things, but a fool wasn't one of them. I sat my ass down and quick. Coley patted me gently on my leg. "Keep cool, Zsaset." He didn't have to tell me twice. I didn't say another word.

As we sat quietly, Ra broke everything. He pulled the stove and refrigerator out of the wall and pushed them over. He even broke the television with his bare hands. He was so out of it; he didn't even notice that his hand was bleeding profusely. All I could think was, *what the fuck is this mothafucka smoking?*

My biggest concern now was Zeta. *What if she startled him and he shot her? Or, what if he lost control and shot us? What would he do to her?* I was fed up with the whole situation. I had been held hostage in my own home for over an hour. And whether Coley was with me or not I was going to do something.

While Ra was distracted in the kitchen, I told Coley I was going to try and sneak up the stairs to grab Zeta. Coley tried to convince me not to make a move but I wasn't trying to hear it. Ra caught us conspiring, grabbed a bottle of Gin off the counter and smashed it over Coley's head. Out cold, Coley was lying on the floor bleeding. I quickly kneeled down to help him by trying to stop the bleeding, but Ra grabbed me by the hair and pushed me back down on the couch.

"Let him die!" he yelled.

If I didn't do something all of us were going to die. I waited until Ra went back into the kitchen then I slid up the stairs. I was just in time. Zeta was walking out of her room crying when I got to the top of the stairs. I carried her quickly and quietly into my room and locked the door.

I didn't know if Ra figured out that I ran upstairs when he didn't see me sitting on the couch or if it was Zeta's cries. But he ran upstairs after me. When he tried to open the door and found out it was locked, he started pounding on it. I was so frantic and I didn't know what to do. I stood week-kneed guarding the door. My nerves was shocked to pieces, even though I was trying to remain calm for Zeta.

"Open up this door, bitch," he yelled repeatedly.

At this point, my only concern was to get Zeta out of the house safely. *But how?* My first thought was I could drop her from my bedroom window. That wouldn't work because she might get hurt. Then I thought that maybe I could jump out with her, that way I could be her cushion.

Just as I was contemplating, I heard a loud crash and wood debris from the door starting flying all over the place. He had kicked in the door and was now standing in the doorway with his gun pointed at me and my baby. I stood motionless and in shock as he walked aggressively towards me.

"Put her down!" he shouted.

When I wouldn't comply, he pointed the gun towards Zeta's head. I sat her down gently and held my hands up.

"Please…please, don't hurt us. I'll do whatever you want me to do," I pleaded.

"Is that so?" he said, unzipping his pants.

I tried to reason with him. I tried telling him that raping me wasn't going to bring his brother back but he was too far gone by this time. I pleaded with him to let me take Zeta in the other room because I didn't want her to see what he was going to do to me. He did, but he followed me to make sure I didn't try to get away. *A criminal with a conscience. How lovely!*

I gave her some toys to play with and told her needed

her to be a brave little soldier like her daddy taught her. As soon as we walked out the room I turned quickly and saw Zeta following us but then she dipped down the stairs. Ra was so out of it he even notice. Deonte had always taught Zeta that if there was ever what he called the 'enemy in the house'; she needed to be a brave soldier. Meaning go find somewhere to hide. In my apartment, her hiding space was a small area under the stairs. Unless you lived there, you wouldn't even know that the small colored box on the wall was actually a door that led to a very small storage space.

When we got back to my room, he smacked me across the face, and sent me flying onto my bed. I didn't know what he had planned for me but I knew I wasn't going down without a fight. All I kept thinking about was getting back to my daughter. I knew she was confused about what was going on. I closed my eyes and prayed like I never prayed before. That was until I heard Ra say after he was finished with me he was going to rape my precious baby.

Mothafucka, you gonna do what, I thought.

Just when I was about to pop off, something told me to calm down. When I did, I remembered that I had the gun Dolo had given me for protection under my mattress. I slowly slid to that end of the mattress. It was still there, however, Ra had a gun as well. *There was nothing more powerful than a mothers love,* I kept thinking. When someone threatened to hurt your child they could forget it. The gloves were on!

He pulled out his dick and demanded that I suck it. I squeezed my eyes shut and took a deep breath. I had to play this right if I wanted to get out of there alive.

"Suck it, bitch!" Ra yelled. He wanted vigorous action to match whatever high he was feeling.

I slowly wrapped my hand around his penis and pulled it towards my face. I parted my lips and guided his dick into my open mouth until it was against the back of my throat. Ra started pumping his manhood slowly in and out of my mouth as he let out moans of ecstasy. He was so into it he let the gun rest against the side of his leg.

Although, he was starting to relax, I needed him to be a little more at ease. As he continued moving his dick in and out of my mouth, I reached up and massaged his balls. That sent him over the edge. That's when I made my move. I placed a tight grip around his manhood with one hand while continuing to pleasure him. Then with lighting fast speed, I simultaneously grabbed the gun from under my mattress and made one clean shot to his groin area as I yelled, "You gonna do what to my baby?" He fell to his knees and starting rolling around screaming in absolute agony as blood squirted everywhere. My face, hands and body were covered with blood. I was petrified that he would get up, so I stood over him with the gun ready to shoot again if I had to. When he didn't get up, I stepped over him and ran out of the room.

He was in too much pain and shock to retaliate or to even chase me. I was up and out of there. His growling and snarling scared me. I was more afraid of what he would do to me so I hit him in the head with the butt of the gun to knock him out.

When I reached the steps, I looked down, saw the front door open and Coley laying half way out of it like he was trying to go get help. I ran down the stairs just as K-Dog, O.B and their friend Bisal were running in. Coley must've come-to long enough to dial K-Dog and tell him we needed help, so he rushed over. Scared when he saw all of the blood on me, K-Dog went into panic mode.

"Where's Zeta?" K-Dog yelled.

I didn't answer. I was too busy praying as I rushed to the storage area and opened the door. My little angel was balled up in the fetal position asleep.

"Thank God!" I whispered, as I pulled her out.

I tried as best I could to wipe away the blood so she wouldn't be scared of me, by taking off my shirt leaving only my wife beater on.

I held her close and cried. This shit was getting too out of control and I really needed to get away from shit. I was making poor choices and it wasn't just affecting me, it was affecting my daughter, too. That seemed to be my motto but I still was getting into dangerous situations.

I was sitting on the couch rocking Zeta when K-Dog came downstairs. He clutched Zeta and started kissing her.

"You're safe now. Uncle K-Dog is here."

After of a few seconds, she fell back to sleep. Bisal suggested he take her to K-Dog's car while we decided what we were going to do. I looked at him like he was crazy as I was a little hesitant but K-Dog said this was the last place she should be so I agreed. Once Zeta and Bisal were out of the house, we went back upstairs.

When we got up there, O.B was pacing back and forth.

"Yo, this shit is gettin' out of control," he said stressed.

"Who the fuck is this nigga?" K-Dog asked.

"That's the brother of the guy Zsa killed in Mosby Court," Coley said, holding a towel up to his wounds.

"What?" K-Dog said.

"Is he dead?" I asked still trembling.

"Yeah," K-Dog said in an angry tone.

"Oh my God! Did you call the police?" I was getting hysterical again.

"No! We don't need them getting' involved." O.B was not about to call them over to the apartment, as it was already hot over there.

"What are we gonna do with him?" I was not about to chop up a body but knew he had to get out of there some kind of way.

"Don't worry. We'll take care of it," he said, checking his pockets. He wanted to make sure he didn't have any identification on him. K-Dog tried his best to be thorough in a stressful situation.

"I already checked him," O.B said.

Coley and I looked at one another suspiciously.

"What?" O.B said, snapping at us.

"Nothing," I answered.

"Go to the house, get cleaned up and let me handle this," K-Dog insisted. "O.B, take them back to my crib."

"Alright," O.B said, trying to usher me out of the room.

I hadn't made it to the door when Yaya's ass walked in looking like she hadn't slept or taken a shower in days. We all were shocked that she had walked in on us while we were trying to figure out what to with Ra's dead body. *How did she get in the front door and actually have the balls to come upstairs*, I wondered.

"Where the hell is my sister? I know y'all know where she is? I swear to God if you did…" She stopped mid-sentence. "What the fuck?" she said, gasping and covering her mouth.

She looked at everyone else over, then focused on me. "Let me guess. This is your handy work." She shook her head when I didn't answer. "Damn! You sho like killin' motha-fuckas, don't you?"

"Bitch, you're next if you don't stop fucking with me. How did she even get in here?" I said, lunging at her. K-Dog grabbed me around my waist before I could make contact with her.

"The door was open so I walked in, bitch!" Yaya yelled.

Suspended in air kicking and screaming, K-Dog held on to me trying to calm me down. I had enough of Yaya's ass and it was time for her to feel my wrath. "Let me go…let me go…I'm sick of this bitch!"

"Calm down!" K-Dog yelled as he pulled me in the hall-way. "Look, stay focused! We gotta figure out what the hell we're gonna do now."

K-Dog was talking but I was too wound up. But then something caught my attention. O.B and Yaya were looking at Ra like they knew him. Then they started arguing. Well, Yaya was arguing and O.B was trying to shut her up. Then I heard her say, that O.B was a dirty mothafucka. I looked at K-Dog and said very calmly, "We can't trust nobody. I feel like a lot of shit is going on behind both of our backs."

"Like what?"

I turned back to O.B and Yaya. "I don't know. I can't put my finger on it." I studied their body language. "But I'm going to figure it out. You can believe that."

The scene was bloody and anyone in their right mind would've been freaked out but it was more than that. O.B and Yaya were acting really weird about Ra's death. It made me wonder if they knew him or knew why he was in my house. *Did Yaya set this up?*

"Okay, well right now we need to get this nigga out of here."

He walked back into the room and told O.B to help him. He started rolling Ra's body up in my area rug.

"You got some of that electrical tape?" K-Dog asked.

"You mean the grey tape?"

"Yeah."

I was on my way down the stairs when there was a loud knock on my front door. I stopped and told everyone to be quiet.

Yaya kept talking. "Who the hell is that? See I don't have time for this. Y'all ain't gonna have me mixed up in this shit."

"Shut the fuck up?" I said.

She sucked her teeth and rolled her eyes at me. Before I could say anything else, she ran past me when she heard the loud knock again. "I'll be in touch," she said, as she bolted down the stairs. She even missed the last step and fell. She jumped up and fled out the back door. When the knocking continued, K-Dog told me to go answer it but first wash my face.

"I'm coming," I called out to whoever was banging at the door. I had to get cleaned up for this one.

K-Dog closed the door and I heard the lock click. I took a deep breath and walked quickly down the breath. The banging scared the hell out of me when I got close. I looked out the peep-hole and swung my back up against the door when I saw who it was.

...TEN...

Before I opened the door, I took off my blood soaked clothing and grabbed a jacket. I opened the door and pushed Vicki back. "What are you doing here?" I asked, almost hyperventilating. She could tell something was wrong because I was so jumpy but she was more concerned with why I hadn't answered my phone. I told her that I was asleep and surprisingly she bought it.

"And why is that guy in K-Dog's car with Zeta?"

Oh shit, I was so caught up with Yaya's ass I forgot all about my child. I told her K-Dog came over and I was going to go stay the night at his house so K-Dog's friend Bisal took her to the car with him. I kept looking around for the police to drive up or Yaya's ass to jump out from behind the bushes. My hands were shaking so bad I couldn't control them. My voice kept cracking and Vicki picked up on it.

"What the hell is wrong with you?" she asked, her eyebrows furrowed.

"As a matter of fact, are you busy tonight? Do you think you can take her so I can get a few things straight here?"

"What do you have to do? I can stay here and help you," she said, trying to come inside.

"No! I got it. I just need you to keep Zeta."

She agreed so I told her I just needed to grab her clothes. "No need, she has some stuff at my house."

It was a damn shame that my child was spending so much time at other people's houses that she actually had clothing there. Tonight was different. I really needed Zeta to be somewhere else because I had no idea what we were about to do.

"Alright, if you're okay here, I'll take Zeta and go but we need to talk about what the hell is going on with you. You're my girl, but Zsa you need some help."

"Okay," I said trying to get rid of her. I had a dead man in my house and she wanted to give me a speech. This was not the right time for all that.

I watched as Vicki walked to K-Dog's car then nodded at Bisal that everything was okay. She picked Zeta up in her arms and put her in her car then drove off. I was so relieved. Vicki was my girl but I didn't trust anyone at this point.

As if Vicki being there wasn't enough, I looked in the parking lot and spotted a cop car was pulling up.

"Fuck!"

I ran inside and told everyone to be quiet because the cops were coming. I stood by the door and waited for them to come to the door. I waited and waited but there was nothing. Then I heard a loud knock at my neighbor's door. "Police," one of the officers yelled. When they got no answer they knocked on my door.

I was shaking and I knew they would see that something was wrong so I only cracked the door.

"Yes," I said.

"We received a report of a disturbance either here or next door."

"Oh I'm sorry. It was probably my music."

They both had a fixed expression on their faces so I tried to manage a smile.

"Are you okay, ma'am? You seem a little jumpy."

"Yes! You guys scared me when you knocked on the door so loudly."

One of the officers tried to peep through the cracked door

but I had already turned off all the lights.

"Okay, well keep it down. It's pretty late."

"My apologies. It won't happen again." I was trying so hard to put on an award-winning act and I hoped they wouldn't see through it.

The officers turned and walked away but one of them turned around and looked at me like he didn't buy it and wanted a good look at me for the sake of it. I thought he was coming back but he got in his car with his partner and left.

After I finished thanking God, I quickly returned to my bedroom to find K-Dog and O.B standing over Ra's body that was already wrapped tightly in my rug. They told me that while they disposed of his body they needed me to start cleaning up my room and downstairs. There was so much blood I didn't know where to start but I rolled up my sleeves, then grabbed a bucket and the bleach.

I watched as they picked his body up and carried him down the stairs. I immediately started vomiting everywhere. This wasn't the first time I had killed someone but this time was so up close and personal.

How the hell was I supposed to ever sleep in my room again?

I had a feeling I was going to be sleeping on my couch for a while. With towels and the fumes of bleach ripping through my nostrils, I cleaned up my bedroom. It took forever. Most of the stuff that had blood on it, like my sheets and comforter, I threw away, making sure to triple bag everything.

While I cleaned my bedroom, Coley and Bisal cleaned the downstairs area. The only blood downstairs was the blood from Coley's head when Ra hit him over the head with the bottle. But my refrigerator and stove were turned over, so food and drinks were all over the floor.

When I heard K-Dog and O.B come back in my back door, I ran down the stairs.

"What did y'all do with him?" I asked.

"We sat him deep in the woods behind your house. Nobody goes back there."

I sat on the couch and rocked back and forth. This was a nightmare. I killed a man and his body was rotting away in the woods behind my house. *This was someone's son.* Then I thought about Ryan. *God, I hoped he would never get caught up in the street life.* This was not turning out good and K-Dog should have known better than to dispose of him so casually. *Who does that?*

"Hey you gotta snap out of it," Coley said. "We're good!"

"We're going to move him tomorrow though just to be sure." K-Dog said.

I looked up quickly. "Why?"

"I don't know, just to be sure. I thought I heard someone and I saw like a flash of light. I'm probably just tired." K-Dog was beginning to sound delirious but I had no fight in me to question them.

I was not feeling good about this at all. I was convinced I was cursed. I should've never left Norfolk because ever since I got to Richmond my life had been turned upside down and inside out. Still rocking back and forth on the couch, I tried to imagine how all of this was going to play out. My guess was we were all going to jail. *Lord, I needed help and I needed my mom. I had not even called to check on her. What kind of daughter and mother was I?*

K-Dog sat on the couch next to me and put his arms around me. "I know this is a lot but we're all in this together."

"Somehow, I doubt it," I said giving O.B a stern look.

"Well, we are. Hey, I think you should stay with us tonight."

Any other time I would've declined the offer but there was no way in hell I was staying by myself that night. I didn't even bother packing a bag. I just walked out with what I had on.

Within minutes, we were at K-Dog's house and I was in need of a drink and a shower. I couldn't believe this was happening to me again. When was this madness going to stop? My daughter and I could have been killed. My fear quickly turned into anger. Threatening to rape me was a mistake. But threatening to rape my child was an even bigger mistake. I guess Ra had to learn that the hard way.

After showering, I laid in the bed thinking about tonight's events. I grabbed my purse and pulled out the half empty bottle of Vodka I snatched from the house before we left. I took a sip right out of the bottle and laid back down with the bottle still in my hand.

Within minutes, I had fallen asleep. Out of nowhere, I felt hands around my throat and a voice yelling, "Die bitch...die," as the hands tried to choke the life out of me. I tried wiggling to loosen up the grip but he was too strong.

"Get off me...get off me," I begged.

He looked at me with such anger. The he started slapping me across the face. When I tried to fight back, he started choking me again. I could feel my body starting to become lifeless. Unable to defend myself any longer, I accepted what was happening to me. This was it. I was going to die. My body jolted and I awoke, looking around the room. When I didn't recognize the room immediately, I started to panic. Panting and breathing heavily, I felt my neck as sweat dripped down my face. After I calmed down a little I realized I was at K-Dog's house and I was just having a nightmare. Thank God! I thought as I picked up the Vodka bottle and held it up to my lips. Too afraid, I stayed awake until the next morning.

Already wide awake at the crack of dawn, I left K-Dog's and went back to my place. I needed to finish getting it cleaned up before Vicki returned with Zeta. As I was driving home, my palms were sweaty and my heart was beating so fast I was sure I was having a panic attack. I knew I should've waited for K-Dog but I needed to do this on my own. He was already in so much trouble because of me. I had three confirmed deaths under my belt. The thought of killing three people made me press on the gas instead of my brakes when I hit a curb. When my Benz swerved on the shoulder, my heart sank. I quickly jerked my steering wheel to get back onto the road. I looked in my rear view mirror to make sure the car behind me didn't ram into me as I waited for my car to stop swaying. When I regained control of my car, my heart began to skip a beat. I instantly realized that I was a little tipsy from drinking all night and I was emotionally and physically exhausted. I pulled into the parking lot of a shopping center thinking that maybe if I got some water that would wake me up. When I saw the Target sign it dawned on me that I should replace my comforter and area rug. I hoped that they had the same one so I wouldn't have to explain where it was in the event Vicki noticed it was gone. I was also going to have to replace a few things Ra broke downstairs in the kitchen and in the living room.

I spent about an hour in the store then I headed home to finish cleaning up but for some reason, my mom popped into my mind. I needed to hear her voice so I called her. Even though my girls were there for me, my mom seemed to be the only one who didn't judge me. As soon as I heard her say 'hello' tears started falling down my face.

"Hey Ma!"

"Hey baby, what's wrong?"

I had to choke back my tears because I wanted to tell her everything that I had been hiding from her. I just needed my mommy.

"Nothing. I was just checking on you."

"Oh, I'm hanging in there. I spoke to Ryan today. How 'bout you?"

Hearing that made me sadder than I already was. Ryan considered my mother more of a mom to him than me so I was sad but not surprised. "No. He didn't call me today."

"Well, it's still early. Maybe he'll call you before night-fall."

I doubted it, but I didn't tell her that. Mrs. Smith made it very clear, I wouldn't be getting him back but as soon as I got situated I was going to hire a lawyer and fight for him. Feeling that I was about to break down at any moment, I told her I would talk to her tomorrow. I told her 'bye' and hit the disconnect call button on my steering wheel, incapable of talking about Ryan any longer.

Before I turned into my complex, I stared at the woods and wondered where Ra's body was. *What if someone finds him? What if there was someone in the woods last night?* I had to stop obsessing or I was going to arouse suspicion. I gave my body a little shake. I had to get it together or we all were going to jail for a very long time. I pulled into a parking spot, grabbed my bags and walked swiftly to my house. Before I turned the knob I placed my forehead on the door and prayed for God to give me the strength to get through this. I opened my eyes and went in. The place looked so different and it was still a little messy.

I placed the bags on the floor then opened the blinds but then I thought, *Maybe I should keep them closed for now.* I started with the kitchen first. I replaced the toaster and wiped everything down in bleach. I cleaned the floors, wiped down the walls and threw a velour throw over the bloodstain I tried to get out of the sofa.

The fumes were so bad, I had to go on my patio a couple of times which spooked me. I felt like Ra was looking at me as we covered up his murder. *I kept wondering what he felt he was going to accomplish by hurting us? It wasn't going to bring his brother back. Then the question of the day was how he knew it was me?* I reflected back to how Yaya and O.B were acting. My intuition told me they knew something about Ra. I took a seat on my bed and thought back to the night of the shooting. I closed my eyes and tried to remember every word that was said and how everyone was acting. My eyes flew open. *Oh God. I'm so stupid. It's been right in front of my face the whole time.* All the answers to my questions were finally answered. I just had to prove it and I had the perfect way to do it.

Feeling confident that everything was back in order downstairs, I went upstairs. After surveying the damage, I went to work. I washed everything first, then I pulled my new comforter out and laid my new area rug down. They didn't have the same one I had before but it was a close match. I was in the middle of wiping my walls down when I heard someone downstairs. I ran to the top of the stairs and yelled out for K-Dog. I didn't get an answer. I quietly took off my gloves and tried to listen for any movement. That's when I heard the refrigerator door close. I ran into my room and found an empty liquor bottle to use as a weapon.

"O.B!" I yelled.

A face suddenly appearing at the bottom of the stairs scared the hell out of me. "What the fuck?" I yelled.

"What's wrong?"

"Why didn't you say something when I yelled down the stairs?" I asked with an attitude.

"I'm sorry. I didn't hear you."

I walked down the steps and plopped on the couch. Zeta jumped in my arms. "Mommy, I was scared the boogie man was going to kill you," Zeta said, hugging me.

"She's been saying that all day. Why would she think a boogie man is going to K...I...L...L you?" Vicki said with a muddled look on her face.

"Girl, who knows? You know my baby has a wild imagination."

I put Zeta down on the floor and told her to go up to her room and play. "I want to have a tea party mommy."

"Okay, go have a tea party."

I laid my head back and tried to calm down. "What are you doing back so early?"

"Zeta wanted to come home." She looked around the den. "Why are you cleaning up and what happened in here?" She said inspecting the room. "What's with the throw?"

"Ummm...We got a little rowdy while we were playing cards so I needed to clean up."

"Oh...it looks like your trying to cover up a murder."

I was startled by her comment. "Why you say that?"

She started giggling. "Well, the bleach, for one, and

some stuff is missing for two."

I frowned and told her not to be ridiculous.

She sat down next to me and said, "I'm just playing with you. Lighten up."

Lighten up, my ass. That shit wasn't funny. I walked into the kitchen and grabbed a bottle of wine and a glass. I returned and filled my glass. "Want some?" I asked, offering Vicki some of my liquid medicine.

"No, thank you. Hey, let's talk about what's going on with," she said, rummaging through her phone.

Once I swallowed the last of my wine I said, "I'm just going through a lot." I poured some more wine. "Shit as just been fucked up since I moved here."

"Like what?"

I reached into my purse and pulled my fresh box of Newport's. I lit a cigarette and leaned back. "I've just got mixed up in some shit that I can't seem to escape. I don't know what to do. I don't know who I can trust." I took a puff and blew it out. "You know what I mean?"

"Sometimes unburdening your heart will help you figure things out. Come go to church with me Sunday. Maybe that will help," she said.

"Oh God, you sound like my mom."

"Well, it's the truth. We're all going through stuff. They put Londa's mom in a mental hospital. And my mom is taking all my damn money for her bills like I don't have bills of my own."

"Wow. I'm sorry to hear that." I had been so busy with my own drama that I wasn't even there for my girls who sat day after day at the hospital with me when I got shot.

I continued to puff and drink as we kept talking for two hours. Around two that afternoon, there was a knock at the door. I nearly jumped out of my skin.

"Zsa, it's just the door. Calm down. You want me to get it?"

"No…no…I'll get it."

91

When I looked through the peephole, I saw a white middle-aged woman with blonde hair and big titties looking around. Her eyes were blood shot red and she seems to be upset about something because she kept wiping tears from her eyes.

Who the hell is she?

I opened the door and mean mugged her. If this bitch was here selling something she was about to get cursed out. I was in a very fragile state and I didn't want to be bothered with outsiders.

"What?" I said tightlipped.

"Hi, I'm Cindy's mom."

"Cindy?" I quickly pulled myself together.

"Yes, she was my daughter."

"Oh sorry. I thought you were a solicitor. Come in," I said, opening the door widely.

"I'm sorry to bother you, I just came to let you know my daughter was killed about a week and a half ago, they think."

Vicki and I were shocked. Well, actually I pretended to be shocked. I gasped, then grabbed my face. "Oh my God, I can't believe this," I said trying to sound sympathetic. "What happened?" Vicky grabbed my hand but remained quiet and composed.

Her mother began to tear up again. "They found her body in the trunk of a burning car." She broke down. When she regained her composure she went on to say they had to identify Cindy by the vehicle identification number on her car and by her dental records.

"I just came by to collect my daughter's things."

"Ummm…Cindy left here a month ago."

I could see Vicki's antenna raising. If this bitch says something I'm gonna cut her ass.

Her mother had a rattled look on her face. "See, I'm not understanding this. I just talked to her on September the tenth because I was in New York viewing the new 9/11 memorial and she said she was here."

"That's interesting…I don't know why she would tell

92

you that when she hasn't been here. I came home one day and all of her stuff was gone. I went up to her job and they told me she quit a while ago."

"So, she has nothing here?"

"No, ma'am. I'm sorry."

"Okay well, I'm just praying they catch the person who did this to my daughter. She was my only girl." Her voice became shaky again as she headed towards the door.

"I'm really sorry for your loss. Cindy was such a wonderful person and losing a child is every parent's worst nightmare. I can only imagine the grief and anguish you and your family must be suffering." I gave her a hug and told her that if she needed anything to let me know.

"Thank you. I'm sorry to have bothered you. You have a good day."

"No worries. I'm glad you came by to tell me what happened," I said, hoping she would drive off and never return.

As soon as I closed the door, Vicki was standing right on my heels. "Zsa, what the hell is going on? Cindy hasn't been gone for a month."

"I know but I couldn't tell her that. The police would be here questioning me."

"So. It might help them find her killer." She had no idea I already knew who the killers were. "Look, K-Dog and them are here all the time. The last thing they need is the police snooping around. Did you forget what they do for a living?"

"I didn't think about that. I can't believe someone killed her. I mean, I thought she was a little shady but this shit is crazy."

"I know, poor girl," I said.

We talked for a while, then Vicki left. I walked her out to her car and waited until she pulled off. On my way back in the house, I went out to the mailbox to get the mail. There was only one letter and that was from the lawyer K-Dog hired for the case I had against my landlord. When I opened it and read it I couldn't believe it. The management company who owned my apartment complex decided to drop the lawsuit. I think it was more like they knew they didn't have a case in the first place. I was so happy; at least that was one thing I didn't have to worry about.

When I got back in the apartment I went up to check up on Zeta. I could hear her saying some things that startled me. I stood close to the door and peeped my head in.

"Shut your fucking mouth or I'm going to kill you," Zeta said, holding her little finger up to her doll's head. "You are bitch and mothafucka and I'm going to kill you wit my gun today."

I contemplated marching into the room and confronting her, but I froze. I needed to approach this the right way. After all, she was only doing what she's seen. So the blame should lie with me not her. I didn't realize last night's events would have such an impact on her since she was so young but they did. When I stepped into her room, she kept playing. I sat down at her Disney 'Frozen' table and told her to come sit next to me.

"What happened last night with the man?"

"He said I'm gonna kill you…shoot you in the head. Mommy, why he say that? That means you gonna be dead."

I didn't know where to start. I didn't think she knew getting shot meant you could die. *Lawd have mercy*, I thought. "Okay, so when the man said he was going to shoot me in the head, he was just playing with mommy. It wasn't a nice game though was it?"

"Nooooo," she said, shaking her head.

"Yeah, that wasn't nice. You like your dolls, right?"

"Yesssss."

"Okay, well you don't want to hurt your dolls, do you?"

"Nooooo."

"Good. So mommy doesn't want to hear you telling your dolls you're going to hurt them. Also, mommy, told you about saying bad words."

"Like you mommy. You say bad words?"

"Yes, I do and mommy is being a bad girl when she says bad words. I don't want to be a bad girl and I don't want you to be a bad girl so we're not going to say anymore bad words, okay."

"Okaaayyyy," she said, laying her head on her table.

"Good girl. Now play with your dolls but be good to them." I gave her a kiss and left the room. I didn't know what the protocol was for talking to your kids when they cursed or acted out things they've seen but I did the best I could. If I wasn't so scared she would say something that might incriminate me, I would take her to a child therapist. But there's no telling what she would say after all she's been through.

After my talk with Zeta, my phone rang. It was Sheba. I was so glad she called me because we hadn't talked much since the shooting. She was in rare form, as usual. It felt good to laugh even though I wanted to fall out and roll around on the floor crying. She was calling to give me an update on what was going on with Deonte and Nicole's murder. My ear was glued to the phone since I hadn't been able to even focus on their deaths lately and needed to get a feel for what had really been going on in Norfolk.

Apparently, a witness came forward and said he saw a man leaving the area. That exonerated me from actually doing it but they could still say I paid someone to kill them. Until the man was in custody, I was still a suspect. At that point in our conversation, I knew talking to K-Dog's lawyer was at the top of my to-do list. I had to find out how to get off that list and start getting my life back on track.

"Before we hang up, Sheba, what's been up with Brina? I haven't talked to her in a minute."

"Girl, you ain't hear?"

"Hear what?" *What was Brina tripping about now*, I wondered? While we were talking, my phone beeped. Sheba had to get back to work anyway so we promised we would talk again soon then I clicked over.

"Hello," I answered, not being able to shake the conversation I just had with Sheba.

"Hey Zsa."

"What's going on now? Shoot, I'm ready for anything now." I yelled proudly, hearing this tone before from K-Dog.

"We went back to the place where we left Ra and he's not there."

I dropped the phone and collapsed on the floor in shock. My body started to physically shut down, my skin was clammy and I couldn't form a word. I was lost in thought for a few minutes then I went into fight or flight mode. I chose flight. I grabbed Zeta and some clothes, jumped in my Benz and headed downtown to a safe secure hotel.

...ELEVEN...

The elevator doors opened, and Zeta and I tugged our bags down the empty hall. I checked us into the Crowne Plaza on Canal Street so that we could be safe and out of harm's way. Things were piling up on me and it was taking a toll on me emotionally and physically. As I was walking past a mirror that hung on the wall, I looked at my disheveled appearance. I had bags under my eyes and my hair was thinning out. I looked like I had aged ten years. I was seriously reconsidering K-Dog's suggestion to move back to Norfolk. I felt trapped in Richmond and it didn't feel right to take all of my drama back to Norfolk.

I quickly placed my key against the key pad, unlocked the door and walked in just to make sure no one saw us going in. I got Zeta out of her shoes and jacket and sat her on the bed with a few snacks from the vending machine.

"Mommy, I want something to drink," Zeta said, running around in circles.

"Crap, I forgot about drinks."

I told Zeta to sit down until I came back from the vending machines. I grabbed my room key and walked to the end of the hall where the soda machines were. While I was getting a soda and Zeta some water, I called K-Dog back.

"You scared the hell out of me. After the phone went dead I tried to call you back but you didn't answer. Then I drive over there and you didn't answer the door," he said.

"I'm sorry. I had to get out of the there."

"I understand, but where are y'all?"

I told him where we were and that we would be there for a few days.

"Okay, well, if you need anything call me. We're trying to figure out what happened."

"Yeah, because a dead body can't just get up and walk away."

"Somebody could've found him but I didn't see anythin' on the news."

"Me neither," I said.

"Aight, well I'll check on you later."

"Cool."

When I returned to our room, I found Zeta with her arms swinging wildly and her eyes wide with fear. She was choking. I was so hysterical, I didn't know what to do at first. Then I remembered my military CPR training. I sat down on the bed and laid her across my lap, then I hit her in the back. I turned her over quickly only to find her still choking. I laid her back across my lap and hit her hard two more times. The last hit dislodged a piece of the crackers she was snacking on. Her crying sounded like music to my ears. She cried and cried, then I cried some more. I held her so tight I was probably choking her again. It was like time stood still for two minutes. I'd never been so scared in my entire life. The whole landscape of my family would have been changed in those brief few minutes. As she was trying to catch her breath, I was trying to catch mine. I knew from that moment I couldn't leave her alone again not even for a minute.

After our ordeal, we both stretched out on one of the beds. After a few minutes, Zeta fell asleep. The poor thing was exhausted from almost choking to death. And one thing was for sure, they would've had to bury me right next to her.

This was just something else that could add to my messed up life in Richmond. My life was getting crazier and crazier every day I stayed here. The only reason I hadn't left yet was because I didn't want the sins of my past to come and haunt me in my future. Also, I didn't want my mom to have to deal with the fallout of my decisions. If I got arrested in Richmond, no one would be the wiser as far as her church friends were concerned. If I got locked up in Norfolk, it would be on the front page because nothing interesting ever happened there.

I needed to find out the truth about the shooting in Mosby and about Ra. As much as I hated to do it, I had to call the one person who I suspected knew the truth. Whether or not, I would get the truth from this person was a different story. But I had to at least try. I picked up my phone and slowly dialed the number. I hung up a few times before the person answered because I wasn't sure if I was thinking this all the way through. Talking to this person could have huge repercussions but if I was right it could save my life. Convinced I was doing the right thing I called back. This time I waited for the person to answer and extended an invitation to meet me at the restaurant across the street at seven that night. I didn't want to have to take Zeta so I asked Vicki if she would come babysit for me if I paid her. Of course, she agreed because she was broke and she loved hotels.

After everything was set up, I picked up the phone and ordered room service. I got Zeta a cheeseburger and ordered myself a salad. They said it would take about forty-five minutes so I stretched out across the bed next to Zeta, and flipped through the channels on the television until I found something she could watch to keep her occupied. I focused my gaze on the dark blue sky, visible through the space not covered by the curtains. I ran my hand across my forehead and through my once thick black hair and tried to come up with a game plan.

Thirty minutes into my thought process, there was a knock at the door followed by a scream, 'Room service.' Zeta started jumping up and down on the bed, when I told her the food was there, like I hadn't fed her in days. Then she jumped off the bed right in front of me and tried to open the door. I popped her hand and said, "What did mommy tell you about doors?"

"Only mommy opens the door," she said, with downcast eyes.

"That's right." I gave her the bellman's tip and told her she could give it to him when I opened the door. After he handed me our food, I nodded for her to hand him the money. Then she watched me with fixed eyes until I laid the tray down. *She is really hungry,* I thought shaking my head. I grabbed a WetOne out of my cosmetic bag and cleaned her hands, handing her the cheeseburger. Before I could even take a bite of my salad there was another knock on the door.

"Who is it?"

"Vicki! Girl open up."

"Hey girlie!"

"Heeeyyyy. Zeta Beta, what you doin'?"

"I'm eaten cheeseburgers," Zeta said, with her eyes glued to the television.

"You're eating a cheeseburger. Just one," I said correcting her.

"Yep, just one."

Vicki and I looked at one another and laughed. Zeta was a sweet, funny little girl despite all the drama she had been through.

I wanted to ask Vicki her thoughts on how to handle the situation I was going through but I knew she would tell me to let K-Dog handle it. As much as I admired K-Dog and trusted him, he was too wrapped up with his business to handle his problems and mine. I cared about him too much to let him get anymore involved in my drama than he already was. Besides, I had a feeling this revelation, if true, would break his heart and make him do something he didn't want to do. If anyone was going to save my ass it was going to be me.

Once I had scarfed down my salad, I brushed my teeth, gave Zeta a kiss and grabbed my jacket. I gave Vicki the name of the restaurant I was going to be walking to.

"Why are you going there? You just ate?" Vicki asked,

getting nosy.

"I'm going to meet someone."

"Who?"

"I can't tell you that. Don't worry, I'll be careful."

"Now you're worrying me."

"Vicki, everything is going to be okay. This is something I need to do and I need to do it alone if I want to get the information I need."

She blew hard and took a seat on the bed. "I guess."

I checked my purse to make sure I had my pocketknife just in case things went left then exited the room. Standing at the elevator waiting for it to come up to my floor, I could feel my heart pounding in my chest. I hoped like hell I could pull this off because if I didn't I would never get my life back.

Departing the hotel, I prayed things went well. I actually begged God to help me. Whether or not he thought I deserved his help remained too seen. I walked to the corner and nervously crossed the street, scanning the area like never before. When I entered the restaurant I was greeted by a young woman who was on the phone. She gave me a quick hello then asked me to give her a second so she could finish up with a customer. I watched as she tossed her hair from side to side like she was at a modeling shoot. Every man that came in or out of the door couldn't help but sneak a peek at her purchased breasts. They were just too perfect and too big for her small frame.

Once she got off the phone, I asked for a seat for two in a quiet corner so my guest and I could speak freely. She escorted me to my table, handed me a menu and told me my server would be right with me. I looked at my watch and seeing that it was exactly seven, I sat back and watched the door. Fifteen minutes later and after the server had been to the table twice to take my order, my guest finally showed up.

"Have a seat," I said, pointing to the chair in front of me.

"Ummmm…this must be good. I can't believe you called me and said you want to meet."

"Well, I needed answers and I figured; if-you help me,

I'll help you," I said.

"So, tell me how you think I can help you? Wait…wait…wait, why would I help you?"

"Because, I'm about to save your life and I need you to help me do the same." I leaned forward, meaning business.

She sucked her teeth real hard, then stopped a server and asked for a Henny on the rocks.

"Henny?" the server asked, looking stumped.

"See, this why I don't like these bougie ass restaurants."

I didn't want to make a scene so I told the server to just bring us two Hennessey's on the rocks, even though I didn't plan on drinking mine.

"Bitch, is you tryin' to kill me or sumthin' cause you bein' a lil too nice for somebody I can't stand."

The ebonics confused me but the green weave confused me even more. I was trying to figure out who the hell told her it was cute but then again what did I expect from this tacky bitch. *Zsaset, get back on track,* I thought.

"So, what can Yaya do for yo' stank ass Miss Husband Stealer."

I looked up at the ceiling and ran my hand down my face rubbing off some of Mac foundation.

"First of all, I didn't steal your husband. He told me you two were getting divorced."

"Girl bye, he was still married."

"Hmmm…okay Yaya, I didn't come here to argue with you. I need you to tell me what you know about Ra."

She started laughing. She continued to laugh so hard she almost fell out of her seat. I jumped up and grabbed my stuff. "Fine, you don't have to tell me just like I don't have to tell you your husband is planning to kill your wack ass." I didn't want to go there so quickly but I had to make her want to hear what I had to say.

She grabbed me by the arm. "Whoa, that mothafucka tryin' to off me? Shit bout to get real now. Sit yo' bougie ass back down and spill yo' guts."

"Oh, now I have your attention?"

"Oh baby, you definitely got Yaya's attention now. Come on, sit back down. I wanna hear this shit here and bitch you betta not be playin' no games."

I sat back down. "I swear on my kids it's the truth but I'm not going to tell you anything until you tell me who Ra is."

"Zsaset, for you to be so smart, you dumb as hell, girl." The server placed our drinks on our napkins. She picked up the glass of henny and took it to the head then slammed the glass on the table. After wiping her mouth with her hand she continued talking. "Didn't you think it was funny that some guys came in the house to rob it right when y'all were there?"

"No, that could've been a coincidence."

"No, it's called havin' a alibi." She shook her head. "Let me guess. Before y'all went in, O.B told you to hold his gun."

My eyes widening up told her she was right. "What a minute? Are you telling me this was all a setup?"

Instead of answering this chick broke out and started rapping Big Sean's song. "I got a million trillion things I'd rather fuckin' do, Than to be fuckin' with you, lil stupid ass, I don't give a fuck. I ain't fuckin' with you."

"Yaya focus!" I yelled.

"Bitch, what you want me to do, spell it out for you? You bougie bitches need to get hip to the game." When I gave her an annoyed look she answered 'yes.' "Yeah, dumb ass, you got played and your new boyfriend K-Dog got played and still gettin' played."

I rolled my eyes at her and then took a moment for all of this to register.

"I can see you're perplexed by this." My jaw dropped. "Oh, bitch you ain't the only one that know big words." She broke out in laughter. "Naw, I heard somebody say that one time," she said amused. "Let me break it down for you in a language you might understand. See, my darling husband has done this before. When he's in a pinch, he gets someone to rob the spot."

I was seeing red. I couldn't think straight or even talk. When I sat there for a few minutes, still not talking, she called for the server again and ordered two more drinks. "Looks like you could use this one," she said, handing me a drink. "Oh wait, you didn't even drink your first one." Yaya slid my glass her way and downed that one, too.

"I can't believe this."

"Well, believe it hunty. That nigga ain't shit…ain't never been shit…and ain't gon ever be shit. He don't care bout nobody but his self. That's why Yaya holds that nigga by the balls and I squeezes them tight."

I asked her if K-Dog knew and she said that he didn't. "He doesn't know a lot of stuff bout O.B. While I'm in a snitchin' mood may I add one thing that will make K-Dog kill him?" She thought about then said, Nawww…I'll hold on to that valuable piece of information."

"What is it?"

"Dammnnn, you askin' a lot of fuckin' questions. Bitch, you actin' like we girlfriends now. I'm not bout to tell you everythin' I got on that nigga."

"Okay, so tell how O.B pulled off these robberies?"

She looked around for the server who was already on his way over. She grabbed her drinks then told him it was about time. "I don't know why I'm doin' this but after I tell you this then you have to do sumthin' for me." She gulped her drink down and waited for me to reply. She was feeling good so that must have been the reason.

"Fine. Deal."

"Okay…let me see. Well, he gets someone to rob the trap house in Mosby because it makes the most money. He makes sure he's there so he'll know how much money and drugs they've takin'. He always gives the dumb bitches he's with his gun so people won't be wonderin' why he ain't shoot the robbers."

I was starting to feel sick to my stomach but I needed to hear the rest. Even if it meant throwing up right there at the table.

"Go on," I said.

"See Zsa, you got me twisted. Don't nobody tell Yaya when to go or when to stop. Yaya is her own fuckin' boss. Got it?" she said, moving to the edge of her seat.

"You're right…you're right…sorry."

"See my guess is… he wasn't expectin' you to start blazin' cause none of the other bitches he would have with him would be bold enough to start poppin' off. That shit there… fucked up his whole plan."

I wasn't sure at the time if Yaya was telling me the truth but after I went over every word O.B said to me that night and reflected on his actions while we were being robbed, made it all came together. After going over it and over it in my head it was starting to make sense. He did give me his gun and he told me not to move. If I had the gun, why wouldn't you want me to come help? *That bastard!*

"What about Ra?"

She shot me a look. "Sorry," I said. "I forgot you was supposed to be in charge."

"Ra, is O.B's boy from Brooklyn. My guess is O.B blamed everything on you and that's why he was about to kill yo' ass."

This story was so unbelievable but it was true. I felt like the dumbest person on the earth. O.B watched me cry and worry about this and he set the whole thing up. I almost died. Not to mention that animal Ra was going to rape my baby after he was done with me.

"I can see the little wheels turnin' in your head so let me help you out." She leaned across the table. "I have a million dollar life insurance policy on him. You take him out. I'll give you three hundred g's."

"What?" I could feel the bile rising so I started swallowing to keep from throwing up. "What the hell is wrong with you? I'm not murdering anyone."

"Bitch, like you ain't done it before!"

I didn't think about it that way. I had murdered three men but that was different.

"You think I don't know he wants to kill me? Why do you think I have my son in hiding?" I didn't respond. "If he knew where my son was I would be dead. So I need to get rid of him first. And you should want to kill his ass. Look what he put you through."

She was right. He turned my life upside down and he had to pay for that. This would've been the perfect time to tell Yaya they killed Lina but I still didn't trust her ass enough to give her that kind of information.

I sat in a daze for a few minutes and thought about. This man played me like a piano and I couldn't let him get away with it. "I'll do it!" I said, taking her last drink and throwing it back.

...TWELVE...

"Fuck, fuck, fuck." There, I said it. Cursing was something I was trying to stop doing but it felt good and went right along with my drinking and smoking. I had so many emotions going on at the same time. I was angry, bitter, scared and downright miserable. The very thing I was in trouble for, I had just agreed to do for Yaya. I also was scared that Yaya was trying to set me up. I didn't trust her and I'm sure she didn't trust me either. But there was one thing we did agree on; O.B wasn't shit. I contemplated telling K-Dog, but I wanted to be the one to get justice after what he did to me. I kept thinking about how I was going to face O.B and not shoot his ass in the head on sight. I didn't want to act hastily. I needed time to come up with the perfect plan to get rid of O.B, all while keeping my hands clean. Then I was going to suggest to K-Dog ways to get rid of Yaya while still making her think we were allies.

I hurried back to the hotel where I was staying, paid Vicki and got between the sheets with Zeta. I didn't even go to sleep that night. My mind was on overload. When the sun came up, I tried tearing away from my dark thoughts long enough to enjoy a nice breakfast with Zeta. I ordered pancakes and bacon for us both. But then Zeta changed her mind and wanted a waffle so I had to call room service back and change my order.

When the food got to the room, my stomach started to

rumble because of the smell, plus my nerves were on edge. I took off the plastic wrap and cut Zeta's waffle into small pieces. She didn't even wait for me to give her a fork. Instead, she used her fingers. After she would put a piece in her mouth she would twirl around like a ballerina.

"Zeta, sit down before you choke again," she stopped, looked at me and said, "I'm not gonna choke, Mommy."

"Yes, you are. Sit your butt down," I yelled chastising her.

Her faced dropped as she sat down at the desk in the room and finished her food. I grabbed my plate and sat on the bed next to the night stand. I picked up the remote and turned on the television to watch the news. I was already depressed and hearing all these horror stories made me even more depressed. Eating and checking my Facebook posts, I immediately popped my head up and towards the television when I heard the female anchor say the police found a dead body near my complex. I turned the volume up and stood close to the television set. I didn't want to miss a word of what she was saying.

I took a deep bracing breath when they displayed a photo of the back of my apartment. "Oh my God!" I listened carefully to see if they had identified the man.

"The victim didn't have any identification on him but his fingerprints were on file with New York State Corrections Department. He has been identified as Rashaad Knight of Brooklyn New York. The police believe his body was dumped in the area. Police also tell us that McKnight's younger brother Darrell McKnight was murdered a few months ago in the Mosby Court Housing Projects. The police are looking into whether the two killings are connected. Now, we'll go to John Reddner for the weather," the anchor woman stated.

I turned the volume down, threw the remote on the bed and paced back and forth like a caged animal. *What if they connected the shootings?* I thought. I was so nervous I couldn't eat the rest of my food. The words 'Darrell McKnight was murdered' kept circling around in my head. *I didn't murder him. I killed him in self-defense. If O.B would have just told them the truth all of this would go away.* On the other hand, if he did, that would mean telling on himself, K-Dog and Coley because they were running a drug operation out of Coley's old apartment.

"Fuck!" I yelled frustrated.

Zeta head shot around. "Oooo…mommy, you said a bad word."

I walked over and kneeled down beside her. "You're right. Mommy was a bad girl and she's not going to do it again. Now, just because you heard mommy say a bad word doesn't mean you can okay?"

"Yep," she said, smacking on her waffle.

I sat on the edge of the bed in deep thought. This whole situation was so out of my control that I thought it was never going to end. I was tired of being depressed, worried and scared all the time. I just wanted to enjoy life and this was far from it. My thoughts were broken up when I heard a loud knock at the door. My heart dropped. I put one finger to my mouth and told Zeta to be quiet then I walked softly to the door. When I looked through the peephole, I didn't see anyone. Then out of nowhere, a woman was standing at my door. She knocked loudly again. *Damn, I was so jumpy because I needed a stiff drink.*

"Housekeeping!" she yelled.

I placed my hand across my chest to see if I still had a heartbeat. Pissed that she was banging on my damn door like the police, I swung it open and placed my hand on my hips. "Really? Do you have to knock on the door like that?" I reached around the door to place the 'Do not disturb' card on the handle.

"I'm sorry ma'am. I'll come…"

I didn't give her a chance to finish her sentence because I slammed the door in her face. I sat back down and tried to calm down as I stared at the burgundy carpet that laid on the floor. While I was in deep thought, one revelation came to me. Now that Ra was really dead I could go back to my apartment and get out of this expensive hotel I couldn't really afford. While Zeta finished up her breakfast, I packed our belongings up. Fortunately for me, I had only paid for one night. I also could not go another night without drinking and smoking. I loved Zeta too much to drink and drive but being at that hotel had my nerves shot and I was ready to feel numb.

All ready to go, we got on the elevator and headed to the lobby. I checked out then made my way to my car. With Zeta safely secured in her booster seat, we drove out of the hotel parking lot. I drove into the center of the city and made a right turn on Hull Street which led to my apartment. No sooner did we pull into my complex, Dolo was seen riding up on my bumper. *What the fuck is wrong with him? Omg, if he hits the back of my car, I'm going to fry his ass.*

I quickly pulled into a space and jumped out. When I walked up to the driver's side, Dolo rolled down the window and smiled. "Hey Ma!"

"Are you crazy? My daughter is sitting in the back of my car and you riding up on me like that?" I said, hitting him in the face.

He got out and grabbed me roughly by the arm. I screamed out in pain. "Aaaahhhh!" he said, mocking me.

"Let me go, lunatic!"

"Oh, so now I'm a lunatic. Was I a lunatic when I was paying your damn bills?" he said, throwing me up against his car. He grabbed my face when I gave him a look of disgust. He yelled at me. "Do you know what I've done for us to be together? And this is how you repay me. You call me nasty names."

I stared him in the eyes and they were cold as ice. When he rolled his eyes and leaned back, intoxicated, I looked over to see Zeta sitting in the car and playing with her doll.

When he moved closer to me, I could smell the stench of alcohol on his breath as he said, "I got rid of that pesky husband of yours and the half breed bitch he was fuckin'.

He pulled Deonte's dog tags with Zeta's name and birthdate on the back out of his pockets. My body started shaking and I couldn't speak. I was so shocked at his confession. I was scared to even move because he was drunk and so angry at me. I tried my best to keep him calm because he had already shot me and killed Quan, Deonte and Nicole so it was no telling what he'd do next.

"I know you probably thought Deonte was a threat to our relationship, but he wasn't. That was my daughter's father. Why would you do something like that?" I stood frozen.

He started screaming at the top of his lungs at me because he felt like I was still defending Deonte. This dude was a time bomb waiting to explode. By this time, my neighbors started congregating in the courtyard. *Where were all these nosy ass people when I was about to get raped?*

When Zeta started yelling," Mommy!" he told me to go get her.

"No, she's fine." I looked in the backseat and told Zeta I would be right there. "Dolo, why did you do this? I almost went to jail for this."

"Oh, stop being so damn dramatic. They just asked you a few questions."

I got so angry I forgot about being scared. "They came to my job and asked me questions, then I got fired. My daughter hasn't been able to get any of her father's death benefits. They know I didn't do it personally but they think I had someone do it for me."

Can you believe this mothafucka started licking his lips? This was turning him on. Okay, I guess you'll be next on my list. Yaya called me dumb before, but I was far from dumb.

"You know, let's go inside before someone calls the police."

"You serious?" he asked.

"Yeah. Come on." I played it off like the altercation did not bother me one bit.

It was a long walk to my apartment even though it was only a few feet away from where I was parked. I was plotting the whole time. I unlocked the door, walked in, laid my purse on

111

the counter and told Zeta to go upstairs with me. Once upstairs, I told her to take a nap. She fussed a little but when she saw I was about to tear her ass up, she jumped in the bed. I went in my room, pulled out the blood soaked towel that held the gun I used to kill Ra and pulled it out of the plastic bag I put it in. The sight of the blood made me nauseous, but I had to just suck it up and do what I needed to do. I went into my bathroom and grabbed the plastic gloves that were with my other medical supplies. Cleaning the gun was one thing I was scared to do the night of the shooting. Handling the gun made it too real for me. Right after I shot Ra, I wrapped the gun up and had not touched it since.

"Zsa, what are you doin'?" he yelled from the stairs.

"I'm using the bathroom. I'll be right down." I slipped the gloves on, so my prints wouldn't be anywhere on the firearm.

"Zsa," I could hear him saying, as he walked up the stairs.

"What? I'm coming." *Damn,* I thought, moving quicker.

By the time he was standing in my room, I was flushing the toilet. He took a seat and waited for me to come out. I placed the gun back in the towel and hid it under my sink.

"Why were you yelling? I told you I was coming."

"I thought you were callin' the police or somethin'."

I tilted my head to the side. "No. I wasn't calling the police. Why would you think that when I just invited you in," I asked Dolo, laughing and tossing my head back. *I was starting to believe I had acting skills.*

I sat down on my bed next him. He wanted to look me in the eyes so he turned his body towards me. "I missed you."

"Well, you should've thought about that when you shot me, killed Quan and planted a spy in my damn house." Trying to be strong, I felt a tear well up in one eye.

"Okay, yes I used Cindy to get close to you but I didn't shoot you. Babe, it was not me. I swear to you. Why would I wanna hurt you?"

"You probably didn't want to hurt me, but when you came after them you came after me also in the process."

When he sat not saying a word like he was processing it, I knew it was he who acted on emotion. I remained cool because I had something for his ass. This was about to be my best performance ever.

"Can you ever forgive?" he asked.

"Forgive you for what? I thought you didn't do it."

"I didn't. I'm talkin' bout your husband."

"Dolo, I don't know. I mean, how can I. Especially when if you were gonna be jealous of anyone it should've been O.B."

"Why the hell would I be jealous of him?"

"We used to date. I thought you knew that."

He started smacking himself in the face. "I thought he was your brother."

"That's just something we told people after we broke up. Truth is we dated, then we broke up and now we're considering getting back together."

"So while that nigga was in the room with Cindy he was probably wishin' it was you." Dolo's sad eyes spoke volumes,

"I mean, maybe. I'm not sure. That's why I can't really be with you anymore."

He got up and punched a hole in the wall. "Are you fucking kidding me?" I asked, inspecting the damage. "Alright, that's it. Get out." Fed up with Dolo and afraid he might wake Zeta, I motioned for the door.

"Ma, I'm sorry. I mean, son was probably in their laughin' at me."

I was beginning to think this wasn't such a good idea. Clearly, this nigga needed to be left alone. I would just have to find another way to get rid of him and O.B.

He finally calmed down and apologized. We started talking and laughing like we used to which gave me a second chance to put my plan into action. "Hey, I'm going to go get us some wine," I said, getting up off the bed.

"I'll go with you."

Ughhhh! I thought. "Okay," I said, with a fake grin.

I walked down to the kitchen and he was right behind me. *Damn, get off my neck why don't you?"*

I needed to mix up a special cocktail for him, so I told him to go find a movie for us to watch. Having to be nice to him when I really wanted to put him to bed with a shovel; was killing me. Nevertheless, it had to be done. Dolo and O.B were making me into someone I didn't even know. All I wanted to do was come to Richmond and open my own store. But no, they drove me to become a murdering, scheming bitch. So whatever they got was well deserved.

"Ma, I found this movie called 'Secrets of a Housewife."

"Hmmm…that sounds good," I said, handing him a glass of red wine.

He took a sip then frowned. *Oh shit!* I thought. *He can taste the Percocet.* "I don't really like red wine but I'll drink it," he said.

I needed to be convincing so I gave him a kiss. "Hey, let's make a toast to new beginnings."

He smiled and tapped my glass. "So, can we try to work on us?"

I acted as though I was torn. "Well, it depends. I told O.B I would give him another chance. I wasn't expecting you and I to ever talk to one another again." I laid my head on his chest and his heartbeat was working double time. "I'll try to get rid of him, but it's not going to be easy. He very persuasive."

He rubbed my head, straightening out my hair. "Don't worry, I think he'll get the message."

I'm counting on it. Some niggas will fall for just about anything, I thought.

For about two hours, we watched reality television shows. I fixed Dolo another glass of laced wine as soon as he finished his first one. It didn't take much to get him wasted because he was already drunk. I waited thirty minutes after he started snoring before I ran up the stairs and grabbed the gun and ran back downstairs, plan ready for execution. I called out to Dolo to make sure he was asleep. When he didn't wake up, I put on the plastic gloves. I then placed his left hand around the butt and the trigger of the gun.

Good thing I remembered he was a lefty or this could've been disastrous. I had just got his imprint when he jumped up. I slid the gun around to my back. He scared the hell out of me. My heart was racing and dropping at the same time. I was starting to panic because I thought he knew what I was doing, so I had to be quick on my feet.

"Hey, come on. Let's go upstairs," I said, trying to stick my tongue in his mouth. I got on my knees, ran one hand up and down his leg and used the other hand to slide the gun under the couch. Then when he wasn't looking, I slipped the glove off and placed it under the couch also.

He looked at his Presidential Rolex but he was too messed up to read the time.

"Damn, I drank too much." He held his hand up again but was still unsuccessful.

"Baby, what time is it?"

"It's three thirty."

"You gonna stay?"

"I wish I could but I gotta go out of town to pick up something. I'll be back tomorrow night."

"Okay," I said sadly.

He kissed and got up to leave. He stumbled a couple of times.

"Do you think you should be driving?"

"I'm okay," he said, stumbling to the door.

Fine with me. It'll make my job that much easier if you ran into a tree.

"Well, drive safe and I'll see your sexy ass when you get back, I said, grabbing his dick.

He smiled and said, "A'ight."

I closed the door behind him and locked it. *Thank God he left because I was not trying to sleep with him.* Kneeling down, I got the gun from under the sofa and took it back to the hiding place on the shelf in my closet. I couldn't wait to see the look on his face when I unleashed my plan. I was about to kill two birds with one stone.

In need of another glass of wine, I went back into the kitchen. As I was pouring the wine, Zeta ran across my mind. I sat the wine on my coffee table and ran up the stairs so I could check on her. When I walked into her room and saw it was empty it felt like something was pressing down on my chest. I ran into my room calling out her name as loud as I could. No response from her triggered an anxiety attack. I grabbed my chest and ran back to her room. I struggled to breathe but I kept calling her name. When her little head filled with pink and white barrettes, peeped from under her bed, I fell to the floor. "Zeta!" I grabbed her and held her tight. "You scared mommy." I kissed her as she rubbed her eyes. "Oh my God!"

"Mommy, I was sleep."

"I know but why were you under your bed?"

"I didn't want the man to come and get me."

I rocked her in my arms and said, "You don't have to worry about the man anymore. He's gone far…far…away."

I got up off the floor, picked her up and took her downstairs with me. We got on the couch, snuggled up together and watched television until we fell asleep.

•••

Awaking later in the evening…. from my own tears caused Zeta to wake up and start crying for me.

In need of another glass of wine, I went back into the kitchen. As I was pouring the wine, Zeta ran across my mind. I sat the wine on my coffee table and ran up the stairs so I could check on her. When I walked into her room and saw it was empty it felt like something was pressing down on my chest. I ran into my room calling out her name as loud as I could. No response from her triggered an anxiety attack. I grabbed my chest and ran back to her room. I struggling to breath but I kept calling her name. When her little head filled with pink and white barrettes, peeped from under her bed, I fell to the floor. "Zeta!" I grabbed her and held her tight. "You scared mommy." I kissed her as she rubbed her eyes. "Oh my God!"

"Mommy, I was asleep."

"I know, but why were you under your bed?"

"I didn't want the man to come and get me."

I rocked her in my arms and said, "You don't have to worry about the man anymore. He's gone far…far…away."

I got up off the floor, picked her up and took her downstairs with me. We got on the couch, snuggled up together and watched television until we fell asleep.

What have I done to my child?

Waking up from another night tremor, I carefully peeled Zeta off of me and ran to the kitchen for a shot of whiskey to calm my nerves. Considering the deep breathing techniques my mom reminded me of, I managed to get a few out but the room started to spin and getting in my bed seemed like a better idea. Just as I hoisted Zeta over my shoulders and made it halfway to the bed, a knock at the door startled me. *Who the fuck is bold enough to bang on my door this late at night?*

I grabbed my mace, the only weapon I had at the time worth a damn and headed for the door. When I looked through the peephole, nobody was there. I dared not open the door in case someone were to storm right in for me, seeking revenge for any of the wrongs I'd done.

Turning away but feeling a presence, I looked through the peephole once more to spot a person running through the darkness, dressed in all black.

...THIRTEEN...

I was awakened the next morning by loud knocks on my door. At first, I thought I was dreaming until the banging got louder and more frequent. *Someone is about to get cussed out for sure,* I thought as I jumped out of my bed and ran down the stairs. I didn't even bother looking through the peephole. I just unlocked the door and slung it open.

I stood there for a moment. "Why are knocking on my damn door like you're the police?"

"I'm sorry but did you see the news?"

"What? No why?"

She frantically walked in and pulled out her phone.

"You better sit down."

"Why what's going on?" I yelled. "You're scaring me!"

She went to her Facebook page, sat down next to me and showed me a video from a local news channel.

We're reporting live from the scene of a deadly shooting which claimed the life on an unknown man in the one thousand block of James Street near the Gilpin Court projects. As you can see behind me, the scene is taped off and the police are questioning several people in the area. We are asking for your help identifying this man. He has a tattoo on the right side of his face with the letters Q.T. If you have any information on who this person might be you are asked to contact your local authorities at the number you see listed on your screen.

Police have very little to go on at this time and we are reaching out to the public. I'm reporting to you live from Channel 12 news. Back to you Stan."

I grabbed my chest and yelled, "Oh my God!" I was stunned and speechless for a few moments. *Oh God what have I done?*

"Some girl from Gilpin told them everyone called him O.B but didn't know his real name. That's why they said unidentified. They don't have his real name and they need that to notify his next of kin," Vicki said.

I jumped up off the couch. "Oh my God! I can't believe this." I started crying and I needed a drink badly. I went into the kitchen and took a shot.

"Are you okay?"

"No!"

I was crying but I wasn't sure why. I think I was having second thoughts about my plan but it was too late. But then I started to think this had nothing to do with what I told Dolo. Maybe someone else killed O.B. I needed more information and I had the grueling task of having to tell K-Dog that his friend was dead.

After taking another shot, my phone started blowing up. Everyone was calling to see what was going on, but I couldn't tell them anything because I didn't know myself. Then I got a call from K-Dog. He was crying and trying to talk to me and I just couldn't understand what he was saying.

"Where are you?" I asked.

"Gillllpin!" he stuttered.

I knew when he told me where he was that he already knew about O.B. "Okay, I'm on my way." I hung up the phone, ran up the steps and slipped on some jeans and my sneakers. *Oh God what have I done? What have I done?* Panic mode was starting to set in. I guess there was a small piece of me that didn't think Dolo would go through with it. But he did. Now what?

When I went back downstairs I asked Vicki to watch

Zeta who had just awoke.

"Mommy! I want pancakes," Zeta said.

"Auntie Vicki will make you some okay."

Zeta nodded her head.

I ran out the door, jumped into my Benz and headed to the Northside of town. As I drove to Gilpin Court I hoped that this was not my fault. Yes, I wanted O.B to die but after hearing the pain in K-Dog's voice I wished I had just left well enough alone. There were other ways I could've got back at O.B. *Why the hell did I listen to Yaya's crazy ass?*

Driving as fast as I could without causing an accident, I thought about my own mortality. I needed to make some changes in my life or I was going to end up like Quan and O.B. I needed to take my ass back to Norfolk because this shit just wasn't worth it anymore.

When I pulled up on James Street, there were police everywhere. I parked and walked up to the large crowd that had formed around the yellow police tape. When K-Dog saw me he came over and fell into my arms. "They killed my boy!"

"I'm so sorry! I can't believe this is happening."

"I've been trying to ask one of the officer's where they took O.B's body but I can't get anybody to give me any information."

"Okay, let me try."

I walked over and flagged one of the officers down. He walked over to me and asked what I needed. I asked him if he knew where they took O.B. He asked if I was a family member. When I told him 'no' he said he couldn't give me the information. I couldn't tell him yes because then they would've wanted to question me. I walked back over to K-Dog who was devastated and in disbelief.

"They wouldn't tell me anything either. I could've said I was family but they would've wanted to take me downtown and I can't risk that with everything that's going on."

"I understand that's why I didn't say anythin'. This guy told me he heard O.B was talkin' to this chick named Ebony when he was shot."

After standing there for a few minutes, K-Dog spotted Ebony. She was sitting on her porch smoking a cigarette. As soon as she saw us she went into the house.

Trying to choke back tears, K-Dog waved off everyone, as investigators tried questioning people. Of course, no one saw anything and even if they did they weren't going to talk. They were too scared of getting killed.

K-Dog's eyes were fixed on the blood on the ground and the one red and black Foamposite shoe left behind. He was so shaken he walked back to his car and kicked it. Kneeling down on the ground, he let himself be vulnerable and he cried. His friend was gone and there was nothing he could do about it. I felt like shit. I set this whole thing up between Dolo and O.B in motion and now people were suffering because of it.

I stood next to K-Dog's car looking at all the people who were just standing around being nosy. Five minutes later, Coley pulled up behind K-Dog who was sitting in his car with the door opened. Coley jumped out and walked quickly to K-Dog's car.

"Son! What the fuck happened?"

K-Dog wiped his face. "Mothafuckas shot him up, man. He gone."

K-Dog explained to us that the night before O.B hadn't been home and how he hadn't spoken to him since he saw him earlier in the day. He said he woke up at four that morning and when he still wasn't home he looked in O.B's closet to see if his favorite Louis Vuitton suitcase was there. When he saw it tucked in the back of the closet, he said he scanned the rest of the room and nothing looked out of the ordinary.

"I kept callin' and textin' him and he didn't answer. I had a gut feelin' somethin' wasn't right."

"Fuuuuccckkk!" Coley yelled. He started walking back and forth with his hands on top of his head. "Yo, I can't believe this shit. Did anybody see who did it?"

"If they did they ain't gonna say shit."

"Maybe Ebony will tell us something," I said.

"As soon as that bitch saw us she went in the house so I know she ain't gonna tell us shit or she would've been over here by now. That's how there shiesty bitches are!" K-Dog yelled.

"We start throwin' some dough around they will. Watch."

Coley walked down the street to where the large crowd was gathered. K-Dog and I watched as he talked to about five people, but they all shook their heads like they were telling Coley 'no'. A few moments later, Coley walked back to K-Dog's car. "Hey this chick told me to meet her at Stella's restaurant on Lafayette. She didn't want anyone to see her talkin' to me. She's gonna be in a white Passat."

"Alright, let's go," K-Dog said, pulling his foot in and shutting his car door. He started up his engine, and pulled out quickly. Coley and I followed.

Stella's was only three miles from where we were but we couldn't get there fast enough. K-Dog was willing to pay the person for the information but if they came at him wrong he would stick the barrel of the gun in their mouth and threaten the information out of them. Either way, the person was going to tell us what we wanted to know.

I spotted the white Passat as soon as I pulled into the parking lot. K-Dog pulled next to the girl, rolled down his window and motioned for her to get in. She wouldn't move. When she saw Coley and I getting into the back of K-Dog's BMW, she took off her seatbelt, got out of her car and into K-Dog's. He turned to the girl and bluntly said, "Who killed my friend?" K-Dog asked.

The girl looked nervous. "Where's the money he promised me first?"

Coley let out a deep sigh and then handed the girl two crisp hundred dollar bills over the headrest. "Talk!" Coley yelled frustrated.

I put my hand on Coley's lap and told him to calm down.

"We know this is hard for you but we really need to know what happened to our friend," I said trying to gain the girls confidence.

"Look, y'all can't tell nobody I told y'all this cause he'll kill me even though I don't live out there. I was stayin' over my friend's house and we all were outside when it happened." She paused for a second. "It was Dolo."

My heart started to beat double time. I couldn't believe he really did it. If he killed O.B to be with me, what would he do to me when he found out that I was just playing him?

"So, did you see it?" Coley yelled.

"Yeah, we saw when he pulled up. Then he was talkin' to this guy who sell drugs out there but then he backed up and got out of his car?"

"What kind of car was it?" K-Dog asked, interrupting the young girl.

"It was a black Benz with rims on it."

"What he do when he got out of the car?" Coley asked.

"He walked behind the buildings and then he came up behind him and shot him like five times."

K-Dog's temperature started to rise. "What was my friend doing before he shot him?"

"He was talkin' to this thot named Ebony." K-Dog shook his head. "She was standin' right there so she saw him when he shot yo' friend. Everyone in Gilpin Court knows who Dolo is and they knows he means business. They can be standing right next to him when he kills someone but they not gonna tell the police shit. No one ever snitches on him because they don't wanna be next."

She went on to tell us that Dolo shot O.B in the back of the leg first. She said the people who were outside took cover. They were screaming and running for their lives.

"So, they weren't arguin' or nothin? He just shot him," Coley said from the back seat.

"Not at first. After he shot him in the leg and he fell to the ground they were arguin' bout somethin'. We ran in the house but we could hear the other shots."

"What were they arguin' bout?" K-Dog asked.

Please God don't let her tell them they were arguing about me, I thought.

"I don't know."

K-Dog's mind wondered to what they could've been arguing about.

"Is that it? I gotta get back."

"Yeah, thanks," K-Dog said, handing the girl three hundred more dollars. The girl looked around to make sure she didn't see anyone she knew before she exited K-Dog's car. She then jumped into her car and peeled out of the parking lot.

K-Dog hit the steering wheel pissed from the information the girl gave us.

"That nigga killed two of my boys!" He slammed his hand on the steering wheel again then broke down in tears. I got out and jumped to the front seat. I rubbed his hand as he cried all the while telling him that everything was going to be okay. Even though I wasn't quite sure it was. He and O.B were the best of friends but like most friends they had their share of disagreements. Most of them were about O.B letting women get him sidetracked from taking care of business.

"God, that nigga usually on point when he in the streets. He knew he was in Dolo's territory. Why would he let his guard down like that?" Coley asked.

"Son, I can't call it. Not unless that bitch Ebony set him up. I can tell you one thing. That nigga Dolo is a dead man and anyone associated with him is goin' to die."

That would sure make my life so much better, I thought.

"I gotta call his family and let Yaya know so she can go get his body and take him to New York. I need you to go get those lil dudes from off the block and let them know what happened. Then all y'all meet me back at the crib. We're gonna go look for Dolo's ass."

"Aight, one," Coley said, bumping fists with K-Dog before he got out of the car.

I continued to sit in the car with K-Dog as he flipped through the photos of him and O.B. on his phone.

"I'm so sorry. If I had never started dating him Quan and O.B would be alive," I said, tearing up.

He looked over at me and said, "You're right." I was taken back by his comment. "I'm sorry I didn't mean that."

Even though he said he didn't mean it I could tell he did. He was grieving the loss of a guy who was robbing him blind and set me up but this was all my fault. I started to tell him the truth right then and there but I left it alone. It probably would've made things worse.

K-Dog sat quietly trying to figure out what he should do next. At this point, he was forced to make a call despite his feelings. He had to tell Yaya that her husband was dead. He picked up his phone and dialed her number. The phone rang. Someone answered but no one said anything.

"Yaya!"

"Who dis?"

Shaking my head. *This bitch is so stupid,* I thought.

"It's K-dog. Why don't you just say hello?"

"Cause I didn't know this number, damn. What's up?"

"Well, it's bout O.B." He couldn't find the words to tell her.

"Well what? You gonna tell me or not? I don't have time for y'all bullshit."

Before she could say anything else, K-dog blurted it out. "He was killed."

"What did you just say?" she asked.

He took a deep breath and repeated the words that his friend, his homeboy, his ace was dead.

"Ya, did you hear me?" he asked.

She started crying hysterically probably without shedding one tear. It was a bit over kill but it was enough to fool him. "Oh my God! What am I gonna do now? What about our son?"

"I still can't believe this shit happened. Don't worry, my God son is gonna be takin' care of," K-Dog said.

Still crying or fake crying, Yaya asked where O.B's body

was. K-Dog told her that she probably needed to go down to the morgue. She told him she would call him once she got down there. Yaya then told him she had to go because she was just too distraught to talk. The call went dead.

With his mind all over the place, he told me he would come check on me later.

"You gonna be okay?" I asked.

"Yeah. Watch yourself. Dolo is OC right now."

"He can be out of control if he wants but I'll have something for his ass if he comes near me or my daughter," I said, opening the door.

I got out and walked to my car. K-Dog started his car and drove off. I just hoped he didn't go looking for Dolo on his own.

Later that evening, there was a knock on my door. I quickly went to answer the door.

"Hey K-dog. How you holding up?" I asked, not expecting him but pleasantly surprised.

"Hey. I'm really fucked up right now," K-Dog spoke softly.

K-Dog sat on the couch and started crying like a baby. Tears flowed down K-Dog's face. I had never seen him like this and I was hurting for him.

"Man, I need a damn drink and it looks like you could use one, too," I said.

"Yeah, make me a double," K-Dog said as he tried to pull himself together.

I made us both a double shot of Henny. K-dog took his first shot and began to tell me that he was sick of his lifestyle. He said he had some money saved so he just needed to put that money into building a legitimate business. He was tired of running up and down highway 95, looking over his shoulder, spending time in jail and most importantly losing his friends.

I felt bad about what I was doing to Dog. He didn't deserve to be lied to but I couldn't tell him the truth. It was better this way. O.B was a snake and he deserved what he got.

"Damn, dog. I'm so sorry," I said, handing him some tissue.

"That was my man, Zsa."

'I know and he was like a brother to me. We had our differences but I wouldn't wish this on my worst enemy."

K-Dog broke down again. This time worse than before. I felt his pain. I rubbed his back and his shoulders.

"It's okay. It's okay," I repeated.

K-Dog wrapped his arms around me and we both sobbed. I rubbed his head and kissed him on the cheek. I was caught off guard when he raised his head and kissed me on the lips. I pulled back and placed my hand over my mouth. "We shouldn't do this."

"You're right. I'm sorry." He wiped his eyes and laid his head on my shoulder. I think he was embarrassed about kissing me. That kiss solidified what Brina told me. He was feeling me and I think I was falling for him, too. The only problem was Dolo. He wouldn't think twice about getting rid of K-Dog if he knew we had feelings for one another. So I had to get rid of him before he tried to get rid of me or K-Dog.

It was past Zeta's bedtime so I took her upstairs and put her to bed. Then I returned, so K-Dog and I could finish talking. His views on life and being a five percenter were so stimulating, I didn't want to him stop. He was also very humorous even though he was sad. He was just an all-around good guy. That night, we ended up sleeping on the couch all night. If it wasn't for the loud knock at the door, we probably would've slept all day. When I opened the door, still half asleep I wanted to shut it and put padlocks on it.

"What are you doin' here?" I asked.

"I've been lookin' for K-Dog. When I couldn't find him I thought maybe he was here and I was right." She pushed past me and walked straight into my den. When she saw K-Dog sitting on the couch with his boots off she looked at me then looked back at him. "Well, you sho' ain't waste no time gettin' between the sheets with yo' dead friends girl!"

"Yaya, what the hell do you want?" K-Dog screamed, about to take her head off.

"I just came to tell you I'm flying out tonight to take O.B's body back to New York. He's funeral will be Saturday. So I only have two days to get everythin' together. You comin' with me?"

"Naw, we'll drive up. I have a couple of people ridin' with me."

"What about you?" she said looking at me. "You comin' to yo' lover's funeral?"

I plopped on the couch and gave her a deadly stare. "Yes, I will be there."

She told us she would text us the funeral information, slung her purse across her shoulder and sashayed out, keeping up her same attitude so nobody would figure us out. We were all going to New York to celebrate the life of O.B but not all of us would make it back. I would have never imagined, in a million years, the turn of events headed our way.

I Shoulda' SEEN HIM Coming 2

...FOURTEEN...

When we reached the Doubletree hotel at the LaGuardia airport, K-Dog grabbed my Burberry duffel bag and walked it up to my room for me. He and Coley were staying at K-Dog's mother's house for the night. They tried to convince me to go with them to the wake they were having later that evening but I was too exhausted. The five and half hour drive to New York took its toll on me. Especially since I hadn't been sleeping much anyway. The funeral wasn't until the next day, so I sat in the chaise lounge putting my plan into action. The time had come for me to take the next step in getting rid of anyone who was standing in my way of happiness. I was going to finally take back my life once and for all.

I was enjoying a glass of wine when my phone rang. When I saw Yaya's name displayed on the screen, I took a deep breath. I was welcoming the day when I no longer had to talk to this crazy ass girl.

"What?" I asked, with my phone on speaker.

"Is that any way to talk to your partner in crime?" Yaya had to be the most sarcastic woman I knew.

I sat up in the chaise lounge and pushed my hair behind my ear. "Don't you have funeral plans to take care of?"

"Yes, I do. Thanks to you. I ain't gon' lie. I didn't think you would do it. And you did it fast. I guess you can't judge a book by its cover."

"No, you can't. Remember that the next time you try me."

"Bitch, you may have killed those other guys with no problem, but see, I'm not blind. I see you for exactly what you are."

"And what's that?" I asked curiously.

"You try to act like you're this little princess but you're a cold hearted bitch. I saw that the first time I met you. You're a liar, a cheat and a murderer. Oh, I know…you had to do it. Bullshit! You loved every moment of it."

"You don't know anything about me."

"Girl, please. You're gonna bat those eyelashes at K-Dog now and tell him how sad you are bout O.B. Ha…ha…y'all be together right after the funeral."

"Is there a reason you called me?"

"Yeah, I just wanna make sure you keep yo' mouth shut bout our arrangement," Yaya said, getting serious.

"I think that goes without saying," I said annoyed.

"Good. I'll be in touch with payment for services rendered. I sounded professional, didn't I?" she said giggling.

Instead of answering her, I hung up. I released a long exhale and shook my head. I didn't know what possessed me to team up with Yaya but I had no choice. She knew I killed the guys in Mosby and she knew I killed Ra so I had to string her along until I found a way to extinguish her. That time was now.

Tired, I took off my jeans and plaid shirt and put on my night clothes. Crawling onto the bed, I got under the covers and let my head fall back on the pillow. Despite how tired I was, I tossed and turned in the bed all night. My mind kept replaying all the drama I had been through. Around four that morning, I was finally able to take a nap, at least. It wasn't enough to function on but it was better than nothing.

I sat up in bed around eleven that morning and tried to brace myself for the crazy day ahead of me. I was about to go to the funeral of a man who single handedly turned my life upside down. I was going to pretend I was mourning, when the truth was I could've cared less. *Why should* I? Obviously, he didn't value his life or he wouldn't have been stealing from K-Dog and Quan's father.

Moving off of the bed, I walked to the bathroom that was bigger than my den. I turned on the water and kept adjusting it until it was the right temperature before I stepped in. The hot water spraying on my body like a massage helped me relaxed. After I lathered my shower sponge, I cleansed my body and rinsed off. *If only this could cleanse my soul,* I thought. I stood under the water, thinking about how I was going to make it through the day. I was reflecting so hard, I didn't notice I had been in the shower so long. When I saw that my skin was wrinkled, I shut the water off, stepped onto a bath mat and dried off with a fluffy white towel. Grabbing another towel, I wiped the steam off of the mirror so that I could see myself. The wrinkles and bags under my eyes made me look ten years older than what I was. I tried to apply concealer to hide the circles under my eyes but it wasn't working. "Sunglasses it is," I said aloud. With my hair up in a ponytail, my huge Gucci sunshades on and dressed in a black pants suit from the Scandal collection at The Limited, I left my room.

On the elevator ride down, it felt like every muscle in my body was tight. By the time, the elevators opened, I was sure I was going to pass out. I tried to get myself together as I crossed the marble floor in the lobby, then headed to the door to hail a cab. I pulled out the slip of paper and gave the address to the cab driver for the Cornerstone Baptist Church in Brooklyn. The funeral was at two that afternoon and traffic in New York was terrible around that time. I slid from side to side as the cab driver bobbed and weaved in and out of traffic. There were a few times I thought for sure we were going to get into an accident. During the bumpy ride, I watched as people walked up and down the street without a care. To them it was just another day but not for the people attending O.B's funeral. Especially not his family and K-Dog.

When we arrived at the church, I paid the cab driver and

stepped out of the cab. As soon as I did, I could hear the sounds of gospel music. The sounds of drums, tambourines and the choir harmonizing filtered outside of the church. Heels clicking, I made my way into the simple yet elegant church filled with flowers and welcoming ushers. I looked to the front of the church and saw a closed gold, trimmed with silver casket, and a picture of O.B sitting on top. O.B's mother was sitting in front with K-Dog and Coley. She was so distraught. She was crying and asking, *God why my baby.* I felt so sorry for her and was beginning to feel remorseful for what I had done.

Tears fell from my face as I found a seat close to the door. I then watched as one after the other filed in, dressed like they were going to the club. These women were unbelievable. *This mothafucka was having a ball. Look at all these women,* I said to myself, then asked God to forgive me.

By one thirty, the church was packed, forcing ushers to grab folding chairs from the reception hall to seat mourners. After a musical selection and a prayer by the deacon of the church was delivered, I became overwhelmed with guilt. This was all too much for me. I got up quickly and walked out. I slid my Gucci shades back on and walked to the corner to hail a cab. I had my hand raised for two minutes without one cab stopping. I started to grow angry. Then a black Lincoln Town car with dark tinted windows pulled up on me. The driver got out and said his boss would like to have a word with me.

"I don't know you or your boss so if they want to have a word with me they're going to have to do it right here in front of witnesses."

The driver walked over to the car and tapped the glass. The window was rolled down just enough to hear what they had to say. Then the window rolled all the way down.

"Get yo' bougie ass in the car."

I could not get rid of this bitch. She even found me in New York. I got in and adjusted my dress. "What do you want now?"

"How was the funeral? Is it over already?"

"No. I just couldn't sit there and listen to everyone talk about how wonderful O.B was."

"Feelin' a little guilty are we?" My eyes got small and my nose flared. "Girl, you have nothin' to feel guilty bout'. This should make you feel a little better," she said, throwing a duffle bag with three hundred thousand dollars in it. "If you hadn't done it, K-Dog might've."

"You don't know that." I opened the bag that was filled with crisp one hundred dollar bills.

"You right. K-Dog has been on this forgiving kick. You know, love one another in the name of Allah," she said, laughing and putting her fist up in the air.

"K-Dog might've forgiven him but I wouldn't have," I said, taking my shades off. "I could've went to jail and never saw my children again." *Ryan, oh how I missed him. I yearned to have my children with me and my plan was to do just that, after all this foolishness dissolved.* That was what I kept telling myself.

"K-Dog might've forgiven him for robbing the dope house but he wouldn't have forgiven him for his sister."

"What does his sister have to do with anything?"

"Imagine the shock I felt when I learned that O.B had killed K-Dogs sister when he was a teenager." She said he was young, dumb and thought he was a little gang banger. So for initiation he had to murder someone. Just so happened, K-Dog's sister was coming around the corner and they marked her as the target. I was listening intensely and my heart was beating faster than ever. Sweat poured from my head as Yaya continued to speak.

"She was just in the wrong place at the wrong time. And look at the irony… K-Dog was friends with the nigga that killed his sister." Yaya said with a devilish grin on her face.

I was in disbelief. "How could he stand to be around him knowing he killed his sister?"

"See…O.B found out who K-Dog was and made his self-invaluable so that if K-Dog did find out he would somehow forgive him. Girl…my husband was crazy as hell if he thought that was goin' work. But then again, it might've worked. That's why I needed you to do what you did. I knew you would enjoy doin' it after what he did to you."

Hearing what O.B did made me want to go inside the church, flip his damn casket over and kill him myself this time.

"So, when are you leavin'?" Yaya asked.

"I'm flying out tonight. K-Dog and Coley are staying for a few days but I can't. I have my daughter's party to plan."

"You know…I can kinda see why he fell for you. I was watching you when you were standing on the corner and I have to say you're phat as hell."

I was stunned by her remark then out of nowhere she tried to kiss me. "What the hell are you doing? I'm not into girls."

"Well, I am. You didn't know I go both ways."

"Well, I don't, so back the fuck up." I grabbed the handle to the door, opened it and got out.

"Don't knock it until you tried it," she yelled out the window.

I remembered something so I got back in the car. "What about Detective Berry?"

"What about him?"

"Yaya, don't fucking play with me. I'm not in the mood today."

"Bitch please. I can do whateva the hell I want."

"I stared at her with such animosity she laughed then said, "I gave him his cut. He won't be messin' with you anymore."

"He better not! Or I will hunt your ass down," I said then exited the car.

Yaya rolled down the window again and this time said, "Bye Felecia."

I'm so sick of that dumb bitch! I thought.

• • •

Back in my hotel room packing so I could catch my ten p.m. flight back to Richmond, I began to think about Yaya liking women. I now had an easier way to get rid of her, so I called her and asked if I could stop by her hotel room, which was across the street from mine.

"Why you wanna come over here now?"

"I kinda got to thinking about what you said...and I have always been curious about what it would be like to be with a woman. Plus, I know you won't tell anyone or I'll have to tell them about our partnership to take down O.B. I'm quite sure you wouldn't want the insurance money to take their money back. Now would you?"

She sucked her teeth really hard then said, "Okay, come on over so I can eat that box."

My skin crawled when she said it but I tried to act like I was excited about it. "I'll be there at seven," I said, then disconnected the call.

I made sure my call with her was disconnected before I phoned my friend.

"What up?" he asked.

"There's been a change of plans."

I told him the new plan to which he asked, "Are you sure you wanna do this?"

"Yes. She won't see it coming. Have I ever steered you wrong before?"

"I guess not."

"Okay, so be there at seven forty-five. That will give me time to get her nice and relaxed."

"Aigh't."

I grabbed the rest of my belongings, ordered room service and waited for seven to roll around. At six thirty, I put on the sexy bra I had with me and the matching boy shorts. Black was always a nice color on me. I threw on the trench coat I had planned to wear to the funeral but walked out of my room without it. I grabbed my stuff and left it at the front desk. I told the desk clerk I needed to run to the store, but I would be back to get them. In black stiletto's, I walked across the street to the Holiday Inn. Before I went in, I put on my shades and tied a scarf around my head. Walking undetected to the elevator, I waited anxiously for one to come down to the lobby. When it did, I stepped on and kept my head down until I reached the third floor. Once I was on the third floor I knocked on Yaya's door.

"Welcome," she said opening the door.

As I walked into the room, I unraveled the scarf and took my shades off.

"Girl, why you wrapped up like that? Don't nobody know you here," she said.

"You're right," I said nervously.

"Let me get you some Henny to loosen you up."

"Yeah, that sounds good. I am a little nervous."

She poured two glasses, handed me one then told me to give her my coat and have a seat. *She sure ain't wasting no time,* I thought.

When I took off my coat, her mouth dropped. "Yeah, dat's what the fuck I'm talkin' bout."

"I take it you like what you see," I said posing.

"I sure do," she said, taking her hand and running it down my right breast.

I sat down, crossed my legs and scanned the room. In the corner near the window, I noticed a bag with money coming out of it. *This dumb bitch has all her money in here.* My thoughts were broken when Yaya placed her cold lips on mine. She started slobbering up and down my neck like her mouth was a faucet. Once again, I had to get into character so I grabbed her face, looked deep into her eyes and then kissed her. I spun her around on the bed and got on top of her. I took my hand and slid it up and down her breasts. When she starting moaning, I knew I had her fooled. I got up gently and told her I was going to pour

us some more Henny. As I got up off the bed crawling backwards, I kept eye contact with her while licking my lips. She
was so turned on she let her guard down. That was a big mistake.

After I poured our drinks, I took a sip from both glasses
to reassure her. She took hers and in one gulp emptied the contents. For the next thirty minutes, I let her feel me up and kiss on
me while I kept feeding her booze. "Woah, I must've drunk that
one too fast," she said, laughing.

"You okay?"

"Yeah, I'm just a little dizzy."

Poor thing, she had no idea I was lacing her drinks.

When she passed out on the bed, I got dressed, grabbed
my belongings, her bag of cash and headed to the door. I opened
it and let my partner in, who was just about to knock.

"Bout time," he said.

"You see how big that bitch is. It took me longer than I
thought."

"Go…get out of here," he ordered. "I'll meet you at the
airport."

"Okay, I said walking swiftly to the door. "Hey."

"What?" he asked.

"Make sure you slit the bitch's throat," I said, before
leaving.

By nine, I was sitting outside the entrance at LaGuardia.
Fifteen minutes later, my partner arrived.

"We good?" I asked.

"Of course. I'm a pro, remember."

I took the duffel bag and sat it in his front seat. "Make
sure you take care of her medical bills and pay her house off so
she can stop worrying. You can keep the rest."

"What about you?" he asked.

"I got my cut."

"I know you did," he said laughing.

"If people only knew the real you. Hey, drive safe."

"Well, as long as we keep up appearances they won't.

Have a safe flight, Sis," Frankie said.

I told him I loved him and went to my gate to board my American Airlines flight.

My brother...the CIA agent. Who would've guessed? As much as I drove him crazy with all of my drama, he was always there for me during my darkest hours.

...FIFTEEN...

Once I got home, I dropped my overnight bag at the door. I thanked Vicki for staying with Zeta and gave her a hundred dollars. I was too tired to even sit and have a conversation with her. Dragging my weak body upstairs, I went to Zeta's room to look in on her. She looked like a little angel when she was asleep. I missed her and couldn't wait for her birthday party the next weekend. Having both of my kids together was going to be a dream come true. I gathered enough energy to take a shower before wrapping myself under the covers of my bed. The drive to New York and the flight back home alone was tiring but having the weight of O.B and Yaya's deaths on me made it that much more tiring.

It was about one p.m. the next day, before I woke up. Although I was drained, I needed to run some errands. It had also been months since I had done anything for myself. So I decided to treat myself. Me and Zeta, of course, I couldn't leave her out. Today would be mommy daughter day. First stop; nail salon. My long nails were in dire need of a fill in. We walked into the salon holding hands.

"May I help you?" the Vietnamese lady spoke.

"Yes. I need a fill in and a pedi and toes and nails polished for her," I said, pointing to Zeta.

"Ok, pick your color."

The lady went to run water for me and set up the princess

141

chair for Zeta next to me.

Zeta chose a purple polish and I chose a dark nude color.

"You ready," the nail tech asked.

"Yes ma'am. Ready Zeta?"

We walked to our chairs.

Zeta and I sat while our feet soaked in the warm, blue water. Zeta watched a kid's movie that played on the screen. I sat back and enjoyed this moment of sanity in my life.

An hour had gone by and we were ready to leave and head out for a bite to eat.

"Are you hungry?" I asked.

"Mmhmm."

"So, what do you want to eat?"

"Umm, I don't know!"

"You don't know?" I laughed. "We have to eat something, what do you want?"

"Ummmmm"

"Lil girl. Why is it that you don't know anything today? If I didn't ask… you would be giving me a list of places."

Zeta giggled.

"How about Taco Bell?"

"Ummm."

"Burger King?"

"Ummm."

"Zeta! What do you want to eat? Subway?"

"Applebee's," Zeta finally shouted.

"What do you know about Applebee's?"

"K-dog took me there."

"Oh he did… did he?"

"Yep!" Zeta said smiling.

Upon arriving, we were seated immediately. Zeta received a coloring page and a few crayons while we waited for our server. I was checking my instagram page when my phone rang. The screen displayed an unknown number, so I ignored the call. The number called back repeatedly as we placed our order. Zeta colored and I continued looking at all the ratchetness on instagram, while we waited for our food. The calls stopped but then I got a text.

What's up? He texted.

I dreaded responding, but knew it wasn't a good idea to ignore him. So I replied reluctantly.

Out with Zeta.

Dinner tonight? Damn, he typed fast.

I'm really tired.

I won't take NO for an answer.

I felt his controlling demeanor through the text and knew it was in my best interest to agree. Even though he wasn't anyone I wanted to have dinner with.

Fine.

I'll pick you up at 8

Ok.

I dropped my phone in my purse and finished eating. Dolo was the last loose string I had to tie up, then I could really start living again.

"Zeta, let's finish up and go home."

Zeta took another bite of her pizza slowly. She wasn't ready to go home just yet. I noticed her actions.

"Ok, how about we take the food to go with some ice cream?" I asked.

Zeta agreed with a smile.

After getting Zeta settled in the car, I drove off. I had just made a right out of the parking lot when I saw flashing lights. My heart started to beat fast. I pull over and put my hands on the steering wheel. I looked in my mirror and immediately recognized who pulled me over. The man chubby man walked to my door. I rolled the window down and said, "Why did you pull me over? I wasn't speeding."

Leaning into the car window, he yelled, "No one said you were speeding. I want to know when I can expect my money."

I looked at him confused but then quickly recognized the face. "What the hell are you talking about?" I tried to play coy.

"Yaya skipped town on me without giving me my share

of the money. If you want to stay out of jail, you'll get me what's owed to me, or else," Detective Berry stated.

"Or what?" I asked.

"Or you're gonna be sitting in a cell for the next twenty years. Your choice."

Remaining calm, I replied to his smart ass comment, "I don't think so. See, something you didn't know, I've been recording my conversations with Yaya and she says on those recordings that you're her partner. Now, if the chief of police and media got a hold of them, what do you think would happen to you?"

His face turned beet red. "I'll take my chances. Get my money or get ready to send your daughter to live with your mother."

He smiled at me with this smug look on his face then walked back to his car.

I was beginning to think I would never have peace in my life again.

Just then, I looked in my rearview mirror and remembered Zeta was sitting there, watching and listening to everything.

Damn. I didn't know what to say to her since she was getting older and understanding more, so I just let it go and turned the radio up.

Our favorite song 'Rude" by Magic came on and I turned up the music. "Why you gotta be so rude? Don't you know I'm only human too?" we sang. I loved it because it made Zeta overly joyed and made me forget about my problems. Zeta did her signature dance, swaying her hands in the air and rocking her body side to side. We sang and laughed until we arrived home. Zeta jumped out of the car and ran up to the apartment door leaving me in the parking lot. She left her to-go bag in the back seat so I had to grab it for her as she stood at the door waiting patiently.

● ● ●

After we went in the house, Zeta went up to her room to play. I sat in the den trying to unwind. I also called Vicki to see if she would watch Zeta again. To seal the deal, I told her I would make it two hundred dollars this time. She was more than willing after I told her that. I asked her to be at my house at seven and I wouldn't be out more than two hours. I planned on making this dinner date short and then end it with a boom, literally. After tonight, if everything went as planned, I would never have to look at that bastard again.

Later that evening, I contemplated canceling dinner with Dolo. I just couldn't get my mind right to want to go but I had to. After I took a shower, I searched my closet for something simple to wear to dinner. I was sure we weren't going anywhere upscale and I was not about to dress the part. No need to make him think anything was going to happen afterwards. During my search, I ran across a box I had stashed in the back of my closet. That box was a reminder of another deadly night. I struggled with an idea. Hesitated with the details of the idea because I wasn't sure that I would be able to pull it off, but I decided to put it in my purse because I had to do this and tonight would be a good opportunity, if I could find the strength to pull it off.

After several changes, I finally decided on a pair of Rock Revival jeans, a white t-shirt and black blazer. As I applied my makeup, I kept thinking of cute ideas for Zeta's 'Frozen' themed birthday party. I wanted to make that day special for both of my kids so I was going to have a character from Ryan's favorite toy 'Skylanders' there also.

To get myself in the mood, I pulled my iPod out and turned to my favorite Pandora station Buju Banton. I wanted something relaxing but groovy. Before I knew it, it was six forty-five and Vicki was knocking on the door. I ran down the stairs and opened it.

"Hey girl," I said, not my usual self.

"Hey. Who you goin' out wit?"

I almost felt ashamed telling her but I did just in case. "I'm having dinner with Dolo."

"Zsaset, have you lost your mind? He had people shoot you and kill Quan," she yelled.

I told her to lower her voice before Zeta heard her. "Listen, I know what I'm doing. Just trust me."

"I'm convinced now that the shot to your arm has affected your brain."

"After tonight, we won't ever have to worry about Dolo again."

Like clockwork, seven o'clock sharp, Dolo knocked on the door. I grabbed my purse and keys and opened the door. I gave him a nonchalant greeting then we both walked to his car.

"How was your trip?" He inquired.

"You can stop acting like you didn't know I went to O.B's funeral."

"Honestly, I didn't," he said.

"Okay, whatever."

We both were silent for a minute. "I got to stop and get gas first."

"That's fine." *This might be easier than I thought.*

We drove to the nearest gas station and Dolo went inside to pay for the gas. While he was inside, I pulled the little "reminder" I had in my purse out and slid it under the seat I sat in. I prayed nothing would happen tonight. *God, please don't let us get stopped for nothing stupid.*

Dolo returned and filled his gas tank up. Then we drove to Stella's for dinner.

We were seated immediately because the restaurant hadn't gotten its busy crowd yet. We each glanced over our menus. When the waitress came over and took our drink orders, Dolo ordered a Ciroc and cranberry juice and I ordered a Crown and coke. A few moments later, the waitress returned with our drinks.

"Do you need a few minutes to look over the menu?" she asked.

"Yes, please," Dolo responded.

"Actually, I know what I want," I said ready to get the hell out of there.

"What will you guys have? I'll take the lady's order first," the waitress spoke.

"I'll have the steak and crab meal with a baked potato with butter, sour cream and cheese and a salad with ranch dressing."

"And you sir?"

"Yeah, let me get the double crab cake meal with a side order of fried shrimp, oysters and clams, mashed potatoes with extra gravy and coleslaw."

"Okay. If you did the seafood platter you get all of that and then you can add a crab cake. It'll save you about $4."

"Oh. Money doesn't matter to me, but whatever way works better for you," Dolo responded.

That response irritated the hell out of me. Nobody cared that money didn't matter to him. The waitress was just being helpful. He could've kept that comment to himself.

"Excellent. That will be up for you soon."

Once our food arrived, we realized the serving portions were enough that we both could have shared a plate. Since we had different tastes it wouldn't have worked out either way.

Dinner went smoothly. We both briefly chatted during eating but the food was so delicious we mostly sat quiet and ate until we couldn't eat anymore. Dolo did find the opportunity to flirt a little.

"You look very sexy tonight dressed down."

With a side eye I said, "Thank you."

"And you smell good, too. What are you wearin'?"

"Versace."

"Yeah, I like that. I might have to get you a few more bottles so I can smell it on you all the time."

"I guess," I replied.

The waitress returned and asked if we were having desserts. We both declined, but I asked for a box to take my leftovers home with me. We left and Dolo drove me back home.

"Well, thank you for a great meal. I guess I will see you some other time," I said, trying to exit the car in a hurry.

"What you mean? I figured I'd kick it with you for a little while, order a movie on Netflix or something."

"I'm really tired Dolo and I need to plan Zeta's birthday party. So I really have to take a rain check."

A defeated Dolo, agreed to my rain check.

I was rude to Vicki earlier and frustrated when I arrived home so I promised her after things settled down, she and I would go on a girls' trip. She was the only one who been there through thick and thin for me. Not that my other girls wouldn't have. It was just that everyone was going through their own share of problems. I wanted to walk her to her car, but I didn't want a repeat of what happened the last time I left my door unattended. So I stood in my doorway until she pulled off.

In my apartment, I ran upstairs to slip into something more comfortable. I was relaxing on my couch, flipping through TV channels and sipping on a Heineken when I heard a knock at my door. I grabbed my iPhone and glanced at the time. It was ten thirty p.m. and the unannounced visit made me nervous. I quietly walked over to the peep-hole to see who it was. A smile formed on my face as I opened the door. I opened the door and was pleasantly surprised

"Were you sleeping?" the sexy man standing in my door way asked.

"No, I can't sleep, I haven't been able to really sleep in days. Come in. Excuse the mess," I said, shifting Zeta's toys out the way sitting back down on the couch.

"Maybe I can help you wit that," he said, with a devilish grin.

"Shut up. Yeah, you must be drunk," I said, pushing him on the side of the head.

I looked at him with lust-glazed eyes thinking, *some good dick and some sleep is definitely what I need.* He licked his lips unable to take his eyes off me. It didn't hurt that I was only wearing a tank top and some boy short panties.

"Damn, girl, your body is perfect. From the fullness of your breast, to the thickness in your thighs and the curve of your ass." He said, running his fingertips across my skin and sounding like he was quoting a poem.

Before I realized, my hands had found their way down to his zipper. He stood up and removed his tee shirt as I unzipped his jeans and ran my fingers along the waistband of his boxers, sliding them down. When they fell around his ankles, I stared wide-eyed as his dick became visible. I had fantasized about that very dick, and it was bigger, thicker and far more beautiful than I'd imagined. Not to mention, his muscular chest I craved since the first day I laid eyes on him. After kicking his jeans to the side, he reached down and literally ripped my panties off me.

Without hesitation, he bent down on his knees, opened my legs and attached my pussy lips to his mouth. He explored every fold sending overwhelming sensations throughout my body. I sprawled out across the couch breathing in his scent and moaning as his lips ran rapidly against my clit. After several minutes of pure pleasure, his tongue left me and he replaced it with his manhood. When he discovered how moist I was, a shiver ran up his spine. He pounded me hard and fast with a tightened grip of my hair just the way I loved to be fucked. With each thrust, my body shivered and my pussy throbbed. I felt my legs shaking as he fucked me in a way I had never been fucked. I felt myself about to cum.

"Yes baby…harder," I cried out.

I moaned so loud I'm sure the neighbors could hear as I released a glass shattering, huge orgasm that stole my breath. Seconds later, his breathing increased and he moaned grabbing me tight.

"God damn girl… this some prize pussy," he moaned as he ejaculated inside me.

We laid on the couch for an hour then I told him he should leave because I didn't want Zeta to see him there. He told me he would leave but not for good.

"We belong together whether you want to admit it or

not," he said.

He kissed me goodnight and walked off.

I was about to go get in my bed when there was another knock at the door. I swung the door open. "What did you forget?" I asked, expecting it to be my mystery man again.

It wasn't. It was Dolo and he was furious.

"What do you want Dolo?"

"I thought you were so damn tired. You weren't too tired for that nigga," he said, pushing his way into the apartment.

"Who the fuck you pushing?" I asked, charging him.

He grabbed me by my arms and started shaking me. My injured arm felt like it was on fire.

"You think I'm stupid bitch?"

"Get the fuck off me!" I frantically searched for my phone but he had kicked it across the room when I dropped it on the floor earlier.

He tightened his grip on my arms and pulled me closer to him, screaming in my face, repeating his question.

"You think I'm stupid, don't you?"

Infuriated, I spat in his face. He head butted me while releasing his grip.

"The fuck is wrong with you spitting in my face."

I picked up the beer I was drinking and threw it at him, missing by an inch. He charged at me with his fist balled up and landed a solid one to my face. I knew this all too well and went into defense mode. I picked up everything in sight and started slinging it. Some items hit him and others he was able to duck. He got a hold of me and proceeded to wrap his hands around my neck. I could hardly breathe. I reached up and scratched his face trying to rip his eyes out. Zeta heard the commotion and ran downstairs to my aid. Zeta yelled at him, "Get off my mommy...Stop." She tried to pull him off of me. Her little body was no match for him so she kicked him repeatedly. Releasing me, he pulled his gun on me and Zeta. I held my hands up in the air and tried to calm him down.

"Okay, I'm sorry. I'm sorry. Let's just talk this out," I

said, scared for me and my daughter's life.

"Nah, you think you slick. I saw your little visitor. So, you set the whole O.B thing up so you could be with that nigga instead of me, huh."

"Zeta, go upstairs, baby," I said calmly.

Dolo realized Zeta was still standing behind him. He quickly grabbed her and walked out the door with his gun pointed at her head.

"You just stay right there and don't move," he ordered.

"Wait! Stop Dolo! Don't take my baby?" I fell to the ground on my knees begging him to bring her back.

He got into his car and handed Zeta to a passenger who was sitting in the front seat. As soon as Zeta was given to the person she stopped crying. Even though the person was trying to slouch down in the seat. I got a glimpse of the person's silhouette. My head was spinning. *No this can't be. She would never do something like this to me,* I thought. *But then again, that must've been why Zeta stopped crying? Zeta knew who she was!*

I Shoulda' SEEN HIM Coming 2

...SIXTEEN...

Forced to watch Dolo drive off with Zeta was the hardest thing I had ever had to do. I was distraught and half out of mind when my neighbor, the police officer found me laying on the ground crying. Dolo knew taking my daughter would be far worse than anything else he could've ever done to me and he was right.

"They took my baby…they took my baby," I kept repeating.

He ran into his house, grabbed his cell phone and called for backup. He came back out and asked me if I knew who took her. I looked up at him and told him Dolo. I gave him a description of his car and warned him that Dolo was very dangerous. After assuring me they would find Zeta, he helped me back into my apartment and looked me over for any signs of trauma.

Minutes later, a small army of police officers swarmed my apartment. One of the officers asked me to have a seat so he could ask me a few questions. His first question was why Dolo would kidnap Zeta. I told him I didn't know but deep down inside I knew it was because I led him to believe we were going to be together if he got rid of O.B. He knew that was a lie when he peeped through my slightly opened blinds and saw me laid up on the couch with another man. As they were interviewing me, K-Dog and Coley showed up unannounced.

"What happened?" K-Dog asked, holding me as I cried.

153

I told him Dolo was upset with me. I couldn't tell him everything because then he would know I set up O.B. Then I told K-Dog who I could've sworn I saw in the car with him.

"What? Why would she help him take Zeta?"

"I don't know. I can't think right now."

"She might be mad but she would never hurt Zeta. So we just have to hope she comes to her senses and convinces Dolo to bring her back."

He sat there silent for a moment. "This shit is crazy! Why was he even over here?"

"I don't know he just popped up."

I got up and started pacing. "I should've just stayed away from him. I made him so mad by being so stupid in fooling with him. What if he hurts her?"

"Don't worry. She won't let him hurt Zeta."

"What if she has no say in the matter? I can't take that chance. Go find Zeta and bring her back," I said snapping. I sat back down and grabbed my temples. My head was pounding and my thoughts were all over the place. K-Dog held me and promised me we would get her back. I just wasn't sure if he could though.

Because I didn't know his license-plate number and it had to be tracked down, it took a while before police could activate an Amber Alert. But once the alert was issued, everyone was on the lookout for Dolo's car. Everyone I knew who saw it, immediately came to my place. I didn't feel like talking to anyone but Vicki and Londa so the police made everyone else wait outside. K-Dog and Coley left after rounding up a few guys to go find Zeta themselves. He didn't feel confident in the police when it came to Dolo. Dolo was a street dude and it was going to take street dudes to find him and bring their own style of justice to him for this and everything else Dolo had done. After several calls to Dolo's phone, he finally picked up.

"Dolo, please bring my daughter back to me."

"Zsaset, don't you mean *our* daughter?"

"What?" I was a little relieved when I heard Zeta in the

background saying, "Is that my mommy?"

"Let me talk to her," I begged. This dude was showing me every shade of crazy.

"I'm sorry but we have to go. Zeta wants some ice cream." *Click.*

I ran down the stairs to tell the officer who was in charge.

"He just picked up his phone and I heard my daughter."

"Okay, try to call him again. This time keep him on the phone long enough to see if we can trace what area he's calling from." The police mentioned trying to locate him by GPS but Dolo had an old flip-phone he used in times like these. They would have a hard time finding his sneaky ass.

He had me wait a few moments while he set it up then he gave me the go ahead. I dialed his number again but this time it went straight to voicemail. I tried several more times after that but it did the same thing. I kept walking around in circles praying and trying Dolo's number.

I couldn't sit still and I couldn't stop crying. I just kept thinking about how scared Zeta must've been. I just kept thinking that maybe since she'd been around Dolo so often she wouldn't really think anything was wrong even though she had seen us arguing earlier that night.

"Zsaset, here drink this tea, it will help you calm down," Londa said.

"I don't want any damn tea! I want my daughter safe in her bed," I yelled, before storming out of the living room.

I ran up to Zeta's room and laid across her bed. I grabbed her favorite doll and held it tight. Unable to eat or even think straight, I awaited news of where my child was. The police monitored calls from the public, including one hoax telling us, 'Your daughter is dead!' followed by another saying, 'She's alive'. Exhausted by fear, tension and anxiety, I didn't know what to believe.

Although my friends kept trying to tell me to be optimistic, it was hard to because I knew what Dolo was capable of. I kept blaming myself, going over and over how I could've ever let this happen. Meanwhile, the police had put out a bulletin alerting local precincts to be on the lookout for Dolo's car.

Over the next several hours, I alternated between feeling completely numb and totally terrified. I kept thinking how scared and lonely my daughter must've felt. And I worried about the dangers she faced. Dark thoughts clouded my mind. I'd always heard that if you didn't find an abducted child within the first 24 hours, odds are you wouldn't find them alive. I stared at the ceiling thinking that time was running out. I felt helpless that there was nothing I could do.

While I was fixated on the 24-hour statistic, my cell phone rang. It was my officer neighbor calling to inform me that a squad car spotted Dolo and tried to pull him over but he led them on a high-speed chase. My heart dropped.

"Is Zeta okay?"

"Yes, but he's holding her and the woman who helped him hostage in the middle of Broad Street downtown."

"What? I'm on my way," I yelled, then hung up as he was trying to tell me something else.

In a hurry, me and my girls hopped into my car and headed downtown to where my baby was. When we got on Broad Street, there were SWAT teams, police officers and k-9 officers everywhere. We couldn't even get close because the police had the whole street blocked off, so I jumped out and ran down to where I saw Dolo's car stopped. There was a police officer trying to push me back but when I told him I was the mother of the little girl who had been kidnapped he had someone escort me to their communication van where they were trying to talk Dolo in to giving up.

When my neighbor saw me, he ran over with a bullhorn in his hand.

"Okay, I know this is tough but I need you to empathize with him. I need you to tell him that he was right and you are remorseful for whatever it was you did."

"What? I'm supposed to praise him after he took my daughter!"

"We don't want him to feel cornered. We want him to feel like you understand why he did what he did. If he doesn't there is no telling what he's going to do."

After he explained it to me that way, I understood. In other words, make this fool think he was right and I was wrong. I grabbed the bullhorn and walked to a spot where he could see me. I felt a lump in my throat and a sharp pain in my chest when I saw him holding Zeta by the hand. She looked so confused. My first thought was to just run to her, but I was scared he would shoot her or both of us. And just as I suspected, he had an accomplice. But she had no idea that once Dolo was done with you you're expendable. He even had his accomplice on her knees with a gun pointed to her head.

My hands shook as I lifted the bullhorn to my lips. I had to make sure I didn't let my anger get the best of me if I wanted to get my daughter back safely. As soon as Dolo saw me he came unglued. He was acting crazy and threatening to kill Zeta.

"Dolo, I'm sorry. I was wrong for the way I treated you."

Zeta heard my voice and started fidgeting and crying out to me. Crying, I begged Dolo to let her go but he wouldn't. I watched in horror as he kept pointing the gun at her. That's when I lost it. I threw the bullhorn down, ducked under the police tape and walked closer to him.

Before I could say anything, Zeta wiggled out of Dolo's grip. As she ran to me, he pointed his gun at her. I ran to cover her from his aim. From there, things moved in slow motion as his body fell to the ground from the result of an officer's bullet. I scooped Zeta up and ran to safety. Once we were safe, I cried and hugged my baby girl. I held her tight and kept thanking Jesus for keeping her from harm.

"Did they hurt you?" I asked, checking her out.

"No. We had ice cream," she said, rubbing her eyes.

She looked exhausted. But other than that she looked fine. I just wasn't sure how she would be emotionally, after all was said and done. The paramedics came over and checked Zeta out for me. They wanted to take her to the hospital just to be sure she wasn't traumatized by what she had been through so I walked with her to the ambulance. As we were walking, a police officer was leading Brina away in handcuffs. I asked the paramedic to take Zeta and I would be there in a moment.

I caught up with Brina and began yelling, "I can't believe you did this. What in the hell were you thinking kidnapping my child?"

She swung around. "I didn't plan this, I was pulled into this drama but I still can't believe you did what *you* did, bitch."

"I tried to act like I didn't know what she was talking about."

"I came to check up on you to see how you were doing after O.B's funeral. I guess you weren't too affected by it because it didn't take you long to jump on the next man's dick. Next time you might wanna close your blinds."

"I can understand you being mad at me, but to take it out on my child is fucked up!"

"If I really wanted to take it out on her she would be dead. I kept her safe as we both were held at gunpoint. So instead of running your damn mouth off at me you should be thanking me." She turned around and told the officer to get me away from her. I watched as the officer led her to a cruiser and pushed her in the back seat. We stared at each other until he pulled off. I couldn't believe one of my best friends assisted Dolo in taking my daughter from me and then had the audacity to say I owed her a 'thank you' for protecting her from a maniac. Willingly or not, she was involved and would pay.

I walked to the ambulance where Zeta was and jumped in the back with her. I was relieved the ordeal was over but as soon as that one ended another started. I couldn't catch a break from the madness to save my life.

• • •

The next morning, the police came to my apartment to talk to me about Dolo's predicament. I already knew he was dead because I saw it on the news but I still didn't know if my plan worked so I had to hide my true emotions. When he told me that they found a gun in Dolo's car, I was elated, but sighed a heavy sigh like tears were coming next. I would've been pissed if all the sucking up I did to Dolo to plant the gun in his car was for nothing.

"That gun was used to kill Rashaad McKnight. His brother Darrell McKnight was killed in Mosby court a few months ago. So we're investigating whether Dominic Wilson…aka Dolo killed Darrell also." I tried to act shocked. "Dominic has killed over ten guys here in Richmond but we could never get people to cooperate with us. Now that he's dead maybe they will so we can at least give the families some closure."

I wanted to tell him Dolo also killed my husband but I didn't want them to think I was an accomplice. Deonte's mother would surely tell anyone who would listen that I put Dolo up to killing her son. I thanked the police officer and asked him to relay my gratitude to everyone who helped get my baby back to me.

"What about Brina?"

"Well, she said she was on her way to your door to surprise you when she saw Dolo taking pictures of you through your window. She wouldn't tell us what the pictures showed but she said Dolo approached her, then forced her, at gunpoint, to sit in his car. He told her he would show her the pictures so she obliged, not wanting to make him mad and also scared out of her mind. She said she got upset upon seeing the pictures and then he became equally as angry, driving off like a maniac from the complex. Strangely enough, they came back to your apartment but Dolo forced her to wait in the car while he tried to get you to come outside. She said the next thing she saw was Dolo walking out with your daughter. She froze when she saw that he had a gun pointed at your daughter's head. He'd already made it clear to your friend that if she tried anything funny, he would kill everyone. Wonder what those pictures showed, Zsazet?"

He went on to tell me that Brina tried to talk Dolo into

bringing Zeta back home.

"Honestly, I think if she wasn't there your daughter wouldn't be alive."

I knew there had to be an explanation. We had been through too much for her to ever do anything like that to Zeta. Now her doing something to me would've been a different story. Funny thing is she would've been justified. I had betrayed my friend. When I thought about it, I was no better than Nicole doing what she did with my ex-husband.

Once we were finished talking, the detective got up, shook my hand and left. I was finally rid of Dolo. However, there was someone who wasn't quite finished with me.

...SEVENTEEN...

A few days after the kidnapping ordeal, I was busying myself organizing Zeta's birthday party. I was so glad to have something else to focus on besides dead bodies and blackmail. I just wanted to focus on my kids and getting my life back together. I had put my children, especially Zeta, through so much over the past year, so I needed to make this party something she would never forget. I needed her to think about something positive after all the negatives things she's seen. The money I took from Yaya sure came in handy because this party wouldn't have been half as nice without it. I was quite sure K-Dog would've given me some money but he had already done enough for us so I wanted to do this on my own.

The day before her party, I took Zeta to the nail salon to get her nails colored blue to match Elsa's from the movie 'Frozen' and also to match the costume I ordered from a company in California. I also rented the Belmont Recreation center and Golf Course in Henrico County. We had over thirty RSVP's which meant about fifty people were going to show up. All of the work was too much for me to do by myself so I hired a party planner. I told her how I wanted the place decorated and left it her capable hands.

The night before the party, my mom and brother came to Richmond and they brought a surprise for Zeta. It was Ryan. I knew he was coming because Mrs. Smith had already said he could come that weekend but I didn't tell Zeta just in case something happened to throw everything off course. I didn't want her to be disappointed. Ryan looked like he was happy about spending the weekend with us and Zeta was over the moon. When I saw him, I hugged and kissed his fat cheeks until he told me to stop because he was too big. He was right. He wasn't a baby anymore. He had gotten so big since I last saw him and my eyes teared just thinking about how long it'd been.

"How are you doing?" my mother asked, taking a seat.

"I'm okay. I'm just a little tired," I replied.

My brother took a seat next to my mom and said, "It's good to see you staying out of trouble."

I thought my mom's neck was broke after she snapped it in his direction so quickly. "Was that necessary?" she asked.

"Ma, it's okay. Ain't nobody thinking about Carlton Banks with that ugly sweater tied around his neck." I started to do the Carlton dance and singing, "It's not unusual to be loved by anyone."

"Mommy, you're acting silly," Zeta said laughing with Ryan.

My mom laughed but my brother rolled his eyes and said, "Cute…real cute."

"Okay, enough of that, we need to get these party favor bags packed," I said getting serious.

I told the kids to play and then I laid out all the party favor stuff on the table. After giving my mom and brother instructions on how to pack them, we made about thirty bags for the children who were going to attend the "frozen' themed party. Around eight that night my mother told me she was tired and needed to go lay down. Her age and her declining health was making it harder for her to travel and do everyday chores, so my brother hired a care giver for her. She wasn't happy about it because she was used to doing for herself but we insisted, so she gave in.

I took her bags up to Cindy's old room and helped her get settled into bed. I also called the kids upstairs and told them it was bed time.

"Mommy, when I wake up is it gonna be time for my party?" Zeta asked.

"No, Zeta it's still gonna be morning. You're party is in the afternoon," Ryan replied.

"After you wake up…have breakfast…take a bath and get dressed then it will be time."

"Yaaayyyy." She cheered.

I went back downstairs, then poured my brother and I a glass of wine. We took a seat on the couch and I told him about how much better I was doing now that everyone who was giving me problems was dead except Detective Berry.

"Who's Detective Berry?"

"This detective that was in on the blackmail with Yaya stopped me the other day. He said Yaya never gave him a dime now he's threatening me," I whispered.

"Really? Why didn't you tell me this sooner? I could've taken care of his ass."

"Yeah, should I just pay him off?"

"If you do he'll keep coming back for more. Let me take care of his ass."

"Okay, you got it, Frankie. Thanks," I said, giving him a hug.

"So, what's the plan tomorrow?" Frankie asked.

"Well, all I have to do is go pay the balance on the cake. I already gave her fifty dollars so I just have to take her a hundred more or she won't deliver it."

"One hundred and fifty dollars for a damn cake?" he asked.

"Yes, it's shaped like Elsa from Frozen." I laughed but he didn't.

"I don't care who it looks like. That's too much for a cake." He took a sip of his wine. "Why can't she just get the money when she delivers the cake?"

"She said she used to do that but she delivered a cake to this lady who waited until all the kids saw the cake and were excited to eat a piece...then told her she didn't have the rest of the money. She said she didn't want the kids to get upset if she took it back so she left it."

"Let me guess, she still ain't pay for it," Frankie said, cutting his eye at me.

"You got it. It couldn't have been me. I would've knocked the cake over, mushed the kids in the head and walked out."

"Why are you so stupid?" Frankie asked after choking on his wine. We both laughed so hard. I missed that. Like most of my family, Frankie enlisted into the Marines as a sniper. He then went to work for the FBI where he mostly investigated terrorist groups. His superior undercover skills landed him a job with the CIA. I hated putting up this act that we hated each other but in his line of work, he couldn't be close to me or my mother. The people he often investigated or put in jail could use us to get to him. He also used the fact that we didn't get along as an excuse for why he wasn't around the family as much. After we took the money from Yaya, he used it to start his own security business. He still had a few court cases pending but after that we could all be one happy family. If things could only be that simple for me.

●●●

The next morning, I got up early to make breakfast but my mother had already beaten me to the punch. She made pancakes, eggs, bacon, grits and hash browns. When I asked her where she got the food from she told me she made my brother go to the store. When I looked at him, he showed his displeasure with having to get up so early and go food shopping.

"Well, I'm going to throw something on and run to the bakery," I said.

"Okay, but eat you a little something. You look like you've lost a lot of weight," my mom said.

"I'll eat when I get back," I yelled, as I ran up the stairs.

I slipped on some jeans and a hoodie then went to check in on my kids. They were still asleep, I guess all of the excitement wiped them out. I quietly backed out and closed the door.

"Mommmmmmyyyyy!" Zeta yelled.

All I could do was laugh. This little girl was driving me crazy. "What Zeta?"

"Is it time for my party?" she asked, wiping her eyes.

"Not quite."

"Well when?"

"Come downstairs and eat then Grandma will help you take a bath while I'm gone. When I get back, I'll let you put on your special dress."

"Okay," she said, jumping out of her bed.

Ryan followed her since she woke him up. Running down the steps, Zeta yelled for my mom. "Grandma, I'm ready to eat."

"Okay baby. Grandma gonna make you a plate. Y'all sit down."

"I'll be back," I said, grabbing my purse and keys. I walked out the door but then had to double back. "Ma, can you help them with their baths?"

"Yes, I'll take care of them…you go."

I hopped in my car and raced out of the parking lot headed on 95 North to the Glen Allen, Virginia area which was 19 miles from me. Kalico Kitchen came highly recommended so it was worth the drive. I was so excited about my friends and family being there and celebrating my baby's fourth birthday. I had a feeling the day was going to be great but I was so wrong.

I was in and out of the bakery in less than twenty minutes. I paid for Zeta's cake and grabbed a readymade 'Skylander' cake for Ryan. Once I confirmed the delivery time, I left. I got back on 95 and headed back home. I was three exits from my home when I noticed a car driving very close to me. I thought I was driving too slowly so I changed lanes, but when I did so did the car. I looked in my rearview mirror to see if I could get a look at the driver but the visor was down and the person had on a baseball hat. I could not tell if the driver was male or female, just plain looking with a cap on, looking like they were trying to disguise themself.

I got back into the left hand lane keeping a safe distance from the car in front of me. The car followed me into that lane so I got back in the right lane so I could get off of one of the exits. I was only a few feet from the next exit when the person drove up on the side of me and cut hard into my lane. I had to go into the small shoulder space and ended up running into a dirt hole. Then the driver slowed up, rolled down the window and started firing shots at me. One of the bullets hit my back door. *What the fuck is going on?* I thought. My life flashed before me. The sound of the bullet hitting my door scared the hell out of me. Good thing my reflexes were fast and I had a car that handles the road good because I was able to speed off before one of the bullets actually hit me. I was so terrified, I sped all the way home.

Before I pulled up I called my brother and told him to meet me outside. When I showed him the bullet hole, his jaw dropped. He couldn't believe it, and neither could I. Someone tried to kill me but who and more importantly why?

"Don't say anything to mom because I don't want her to get upset," I begged.

"I won't but you need to be careful. Damn, Zsa. "

"I will. I'll put my car in the shop tomorrow and get a rental for a few days until we can figure out what's going on. Right now, I have to calm down. I don't want anything to mess up Zeta's birthday party." I was shaking uncontrollably but remained composed.

"Do you think it was Detective Berry?"

"Could've been. Let's just celebrate Zeta's birthday right now and I'll figure out how to take care of Berry. We better take my car," Frankie suggested.

"Yeah, that's a good idea. I can't believe this shit."

Thinking that something could've happened to me the day of my daughter's birthday party pissed me off. I walked in the house with a fake smile. I had to contain my anger and put the shooting situation on the back burner until Zeta enjoyed her day. After that, it was going to be on.

One o' clock that afternoon, we were all dressed and ready to go to the Recreation Center. The party wasn't until two, but I wanted to get there early just in case I needed to make some adjustments. I had confidence in the party planner but I wanted to make sure things were the way I wanted them. When we got inside, Zeta's facial expression told me that she loved her decorations for her Disney 'Frozen' themed party. There was a winter Wonderland back drop with snowflakes for the kids to take pictures, blue popcorn snowballs, blue smoothies, mini hot-dogs and hamburgers, 'Frozen' fruit cups and marshmallows dipped in blue dye with white chocolate.

When she saw her cake, her eyes got big. "Mommy! It's Elsa!" she screamed.

"That's right! And Ryan what's next to Elsa?"

"Oh my goodness, Mommy! 'Skylanders'."

They both stared at their cakes for minutes, shocked at what Id pulled off for them. The smiles on their faces were priceless. I accomplished my mission.

At two, the guests started to arrive. Vicki, Londa, Sheba, K-Dog and Coley were all there. A few of my friends from Norfolk and a few family members. Brina was still cooling her jealous heels in Richmond City jail so she wasn't coming or even invited. I wanted to invite Deonte's mother but she still blamed me for his death and I didn't want that negative energy at my baby's party. By three o' clock, the party was in full gear. The kids were having fun and so were the adults. While everyone was enjoying themselves, I played hostess.

Once my guests had eaten, we sang happy birthday to Zeta then let her cut her cake. Her little butt cut herself a piece, laid the knife on the table then sat down and ate. I shook my head as I finished cutting everyone a piece of cake. I asked the party planner if she would put the rest in the box the bakery left so we could start cleaning up because we needed to be out of there by five.

"You need help," my mom asked.

"No. Go enjoy the party Momma. I got it."

K-Dog came over and gave me a big hug. "Yo…you did your thing with this party."

"Thanks. I wanted her to have a great time. They're both having a great time."

"Well, I have to cut out. I got something to take care of," K-Dog said.

I looked around to make sure no one was around. "When I went to pay for the cake today someone shot at me on 95," I whispered.

"What?"

"Yeah. The bullets missed me but one hit my back door."

"Why the hell would someone shoot at you?"

"I don't know but I'm going to find out. We'll talk about it more later. I need to take care of all these bad ass kids running around here," I said a little irritated that the parents were letting their kids run amuck.

After K-Dog and Coley left, Vicki came over and asked me what was going on with Coley.

"See that's why we're friends. I was thinking the same thing. He's been acting a little weird lately. Maybe Quan and O.B's death is still bothering him," I said.

"He looked like he was on something."

"I think that's why K-Dog left early. He probably didn't want Coley to do anything to embarrass him or disrupt the party."

The party started to fizzle down and one by one my guests left. We cleaned up, packed some of the items in my brother's car and the rest I gave to the party planner. I told her to keep the stuff and use it for someone else's party. I checked out with the manager of the recreation center then told my brother and mother I was ready to go.

We walked up to my brother's car and immediately noticed what I thought was a flyer on the windshield. I took the paper off the windshield and read it. When I saw 'I won't miss next time bitch', I looked around. My body shook with fear. My brother grabbed the note out of my hand and read it. He looked around too but there was no one around who looked out of the ordinary.

"What is it?" my mom asked.

"It's nothing, just a note. I think they meant to put it on someone else's car."

My brother unlocked the doors and we all loaded in. On the drive home, I couldn't help but think, *this can't be happening again*. First Ra stalked me and now this idiot. Someone had to be watching me. How else would they know where I was? *Once again, my life was in danger and this time I might not be so lucky.*

I Shoulda' SEEN HIM Coming 2

...EIGHTEEN...

Two weeks after Zeta's party, I started feeling sick. I couldn't hold anything on my stomach, I had lost ten pounds and I couldn't get out of the bed. I didn't know if I was feeling the effects of some kind of flu or if my body was just tired from everything I had been through the last year. Then I thought it was probably mental because I was starting to get weird phone calls and creepy notes left on my rental car. The whole thing had me so unsettled, I bought a house in Norfolk and planned on moving back there with Zeta so I could be close to Ryan and my mom. Richmond was getting so bad. People were getting killed left and right and I didn't want Zeta growing up there. This place had bought me so many bad memories and I was ready to get away from there.

It was a Saturday night and Zeta was staying over at Vicki's house for the evening. I was laying in bed when a weft of my underarms almost made me throw up. I hadn't showered in days and it smelled like it. After sitting on the edge of my bed for five minutes trying to get my thoughts together, I took a shower, made me some lunch and then laid on the couch in the den. I fell asleep again until nine that night. Holding the remote, I flipped through the channels on the television. Iyanla Vanzant's 'Fix My Life' was on and I was in need of some free counseling, so I laid the remote down and listened to what she had to say.

Mid-way through the show, I started to feel nauseous. I started to sweat profusely and I felt like I was about to pass out. I quickly got up and ran to the half bath. I barely made it when all of the food I had eaten came up. I made my way back to the couch and laid down. I pulled my phone out and went to my Google icon. I entered my symptoms to see what could possibly be wrong with me. The results showed a number of possibilities but the main two were that I could have a stomach virus or be pregnant. That got me to thinking. I had missed my period but that happened a lot if I was under a lot of stress and I did have a sexual encounter about two weeks ago. Naw…I can't be pregnant. *Maybe I ate something that didn't agree with me*, I thought.

Curiosity got the best of me so I put on my sneakers and headed to the store to get a pregnancy test. If I could rule out being pregnant then the odds were I had a stomach virus.

On my way out the door, I grabbed the trash. When I turned around, I saw a shadow walk past my window. I went outside and saw the person peaking around the corner at me. I yelled, "Hey" as loud as I could. The person took off running. I wanted to run after the person, although that wouldn't have been a good idea plus I was too tired. *That was strange, but I was used to strange*, I said to myself.

I took the bag of trash, threw it in the dumpster then got into my car that I had picked up from the shop the day before. As I was driving, my mind drifted back to all the shit I had been through in Richmond. I couldn't wait to get the hell out of this city. Just when I thought I was over all the madness, it started all over again. Damn.

I pulled into Walgreen's parking lot, got out of my car and headed nervously to the door. I was not ready to be a mom again, especially with everything I had going on. I was still trying to get Ryan back permanently, my mom was sick and someone was stalking me. My hands were already full and I didn't want to add anything else into the mix.

Once I was in the store, I felt a little strange as I walked around. I tried not to dwell on it, but the longer I was in there it got worse. The eerie feeling was very unsettling, so I grabbed a trial size bottle of Tylenol and a pregnancy test then went to the register. As I was waiting to be checked out, my stomach felt it had knots in it. My head began to pound without any warning.

"Good evening ma'am did you find everything you needed?" the clerk with red hair and a face full of acne asked, as he rung up my items.

"Yes, I did," I said with a blandness tone in my voice.

"Would you like to sign up for our reward card?"

I had to keep myself from going off on him. I had Tylenol and a pregnancy test, did he really think I felt like answering all his damn questions?

"No thank you."

He gave me my total and I swiped my card and signed the receipt as fast as I could. He asked if there was anything else he could help me with as he handed me my bag.

"Do you have a restroom in here?" I asked, feeling sick to my stomach.

"We sure do. It's in the back to the right."

"Thanks."

I made my way to the back of the store and opened the door to the restrooms. When I walked in, I got even sicker. There were only two stalls and one of them was occupied. I couldn't hold it in any longer so I used the handicap stall. I was like a volcano erupting. I guess the person next to me got worried because she asked if I was okay. After I told her yes, she left the bathroom. Still vomiting, I heard someone come to the restroom. I assumed the lady went and told one of the clerks to come check on me. That wasn't the case. Instead of someone seeing how I was doing, they turned the lights off.

"Is someone out there? Can you turn the lights back on please?"

No one answered but I heard the door open again. I grabbed some tissue, wiped my mouth and let my hands guide me to the lights. I turned them back on and looked in the other stall but no one was there. I went to the door turned the knob and pushed on it but it wouldn't open. I pushed again and it still wouldn't open. I started to panic. I pounded on the door hoping someone would hear me. After about five minutes of banging and screaming, an employee yelled back, "Ma'am hold on one second."

"Get me out of here!" I yelled back.

A few seconds later, the door flew open. I was crying and thankful to the employee.

"Why was it locked?" I asked.

"Someone pushed a cart in front of it and locked it. I assure you it wasn't one of us. That's a fire hazard."

I was so relieved to out of the bathroom but I was still shaking. It just really shook me up. I wanted to get the hell out of there. I walked up to the clerk at the counter and began to question him. Someone locked me in the bathroom on purpose and I needed to know who.

"Hi. Can I help you?" the clerk asked.

"Did you see anyone else go to the restrooms?"

"No. I only told you where it was."

I looked around the store from where I was standing.

"Can you just watch me until I get into my car?"

"Sure. Are you sure you're okay ma'am?"

"I don't know. I just need to get out of here."

The clerk stepped from around the counter and walked me to my car. Once I was safely in my car and pulling out of the parking lot he went back in.

• • •

When I got home, I threw my bag from Walgreens on the table, opened my half empty bottle of wine and started drinking straight from the bottle. I sat down at the table and tried to figure out who was playing games with me. The only explanation I could come up with was maybe it was Detective Berry. *Could he be the one stalking me?* I thought. *He did want money from me.* My mounting frustration was making me not only physically but also emotionally sick. I took another sip of wine then placed the bottle on the table. When I looked down at the table, I noticed the pregnancy test laying half way out of the bag. I had forgotten that quick; the whole purpose of me even going to the store.

I took the pregnancy test out of the bag and went into the bathroom. My anxiety intensified as the toilet came into view. I sat, gritting my teeth as I opened the box. I was so vexed when I realized it was not the pee-on-a-stick kind of test but a pee-in-a-cup test without a damn cup.

"Are you fucking kidding me?" I yelled.

I got off the toilet, pulled my pants up and walked into the kitchen to get a foam cup. I then went back into the bathroom to start over. I let a small stream of urine go into the bowl then I caught a good amount in the cup. I wiped myself, pulled up my pants and stuck the test in the cup. I looked at my watch to make sure I let it sit in the cup the required time. While I waited, I went back into the kitchen and sat nervously while I sipped on some more wine. *Should I be drinking this? What if I am pregnant?* I thought. I pushed the glass away from me and checked my social media pages to occupy my mind.

It was now time to read my results and I was a wreck. I was praying my symptoms were just a bug or something because I wasn't ready to be a mother again. I went into the restroom and pulled the stick out of the cup. Taking a deep breath, I looked down at the results. Well…that settles it!

...NINETEEN...

After the home pregnancy test came back positive, I couldn't believe it was right so I scheduled an appointment to see my doctor. The day of my appointment the morning sickness became more intense and had occurred almost every day now. I was sleeping all day and couldn't eat.

When I got to my appointment, they did a blood and urine test. I never thought I would walk out of there with positive results. I thought for sure the home pregnancy was wrong. Here I am on my third child, with three different fathers and widowed. What am I doing? I thought. I didn't even know how this man is going to take this news. I didn't know if he would want to be a father or even be with me.

I was uneasy with the news I received and had to give him. I paced the floor with the results of the test. I waited for him to come over. We had spoken earlier and I told him I needed to see him and he agreed to meet with me tonight. He was taking way too long for me. I wanted to get this over with. I had to get it off my chest. I decided to call him and see where he was.

"Hello," the male voice spoke.

"Hey. Are you still coming over?"

"Yeah, I had to make a stop. I'm actually pulling up now."

"Oh....Ok. Well I'll see you in a few."

I stood in the doorway waiting for him to arrive. I watched him park and walk ever so confidently to my door. "What's up pretty lady?"

You have no idea. I thought to myself. I didn't want to put this off any longer and had to tell him before he got comfortable. I closed the door behind us and walked over the couch.

I told him I had something important to tell him and wasn't sure how he would take it. I was nervous and I couldn't find the right words to say.

He asked. "What's wrong Zsa? You look pale!"

I sat there on the verge of vomiting.

"Are you sick or something? Tell me what's wrong!"

Before he could say another word. I just blurted it out before I knew it. "I'm pregnant!"

Complete silence took over the room. I could hear my stomach gurgling. He sat quiet for what seemed like five minutes and just stared at me. I didn't know what to do or say. I looked away and began to cry silently. He leaned over, grabbed my waist and rubbed my stomach.

"Are you sure?"

I turned to him and handed him the test results I had been holding. He read over it and what happened next was like a movie scene. It touched my soul deeply.

"Marry me?" He said

I couldn't believe my ears. I had to ask him to repeat himself and he did.

"Marry me?" he repeated rubbing the unborn child growing inside of me.

Was I dreaming? I grabbed his face and kissed him then answered, "Yes! Yes K-Dog I will marry you." I couldn't believe I had a wedding to plan.

The next day after telling my family and friends, I contacted a few venues to celebrate our special day. We decided to just do a small intimate ceremony with only our closet family and friends. In between calls, my phone rang. I recognized that number and almost hesitated to answer it. I didn't need any bad news right now. I was on cloud nine. Mrs. Smith was not going to upset me with her nonsense today. So, I decided to ignore her call and send her to voicemail. I will just have to call her back tomorrow.

I continued my wedding planning by contacting more venues. We didn't have a set date in mind, but of course I wanted to get married before I was a big balloon. So I inquired on dates over the next three months and pricing.

Mrs. Smith called again that evening and reluctantly I answered. I didn't want to not answer and it is something wrong with Ryan. Mrs. Smith was overly excited when she spoke to me. This conversation completely caught me off guard.

"Hello Ms. Jones. How are you doing today?"

"Hi Mrs. Smith, I'm actually doing very well despite a little nausea."

"Oh, I'm sorry to hear that. Have you seen a doctor yet?" She inquired.

"Actually, I have and in about 9 months Ryan will be a big brother all over again."

"Oh, you're pregnant? Congratulations to you then! Speaking of Ryan, Ryan has asked to come home quite frequently the past couple of weeks."

"I wish he could come home. I miss my son so much."

"Well, that's why I was calling you."

"Huh, I don't understand."

"You have been doing so well and have not had any troubles so I wanted to arrange a time to meet with you to bring Ryan to you or meet you somewhere."

I began to ball crying. Tears flowed down my face like a river.

"Mrs. Smith, are you serious?"

"Yes ma'am, I would play with you like that."

"Thank you so much."

We made arrangements and soon Ryan would be back home with me and Zeta.

Just to think my days were getting better and better. Ryan was coming home, I was having a baby and getting married.

Later that night, I got into bed and turned on my television. I was watching 'Criminal Minds' when the show was interrupted by the local news on scene with the Chief of Richmond City Police Department. They were holding a press conference about a police officer being killed. First, the cops were killing us, now they're getting killed.

Wow! I thought.

When the Chief of Police stood at the podium, I turned the volume up:

At seven p.m., a detective from the Narcotics Division was found dead in his home. Dwayne Berry was being investigated as a part of an FBI sting for illegally apprehending citizens by stealing money and drugs from undercover agents whom he thought were low level drug dealers.

I sat up in my bed. "Oh my God!"

An internal affairs investigation alleges that instead of arresting local drug dealers Berry would take their drugs and money for himself, instead of turning the evidence in for reporting measures. Agents were at Berry's home to arrest him but when they arrived, he was pronounced dead on scene. The Richmond Police Department and the FBI will not be releasing any more information at this time, as we are still investigating the scene.

I was still trying to listen to the press conference when my phone started to vibrate. There was a text message from my brother Frankie. When I opened it, there were no words, just a smiley face. I knew what it meant though. Once again, my brother had come through for me.

I couldn't believe it. He was finally out of my life. I was so glad I didn't have to worry about him trying to send me to jail if I didn't pay him off. As far as I was concerned, he got what he deserved. I was so glad I didn't have to worry about being stalked anymore. I had so much good news that night, I ended up sleeping like a baby. Finally…

● ● ●

I continued my wedding planning over the next week. Ironically, since telling K-Dog I was pregnant and planning our wedding, I was still receiving strange calls and threatening notes left on my car. I thought it was Detective Berry who was stalking me but clearly it wasn't because he was dead. I remember one time I answered my phone and a male voice was on the other end and he just panted in the phone then yelled, "Die bitch!" Another call was a female voice. She just said my name and whispered. "I know and soon everyone will know."

I was beginning to worry about these calls and threats. Stuff like this usually doesn't bother me, but I think since having my hormones all over the place was making me a bit on the sensitive side. I had a doctor's appointment and as I opened the door, I saw my door had been egged. I didn't have time to clean it and would just have to do it when I came back. But walking up to my car I could see a piece of paper flapping.

It was another note. This one was disturbing. I started to read it.

You're enjoying life like you don't have a care in the world but that shit is gonna come to an end believe that! The murderer is gonna get murdered.

I cried in the car. I had no idea who was taunting me and why? I drove in silence to the doctor's. I had to get myself together and focus on bringing a healthy child into the world. I didn't tell K-Dog about the calls and notes, but after this note, it was time I let him know. I felt my safety and sanity were at stake and I was certain he would want to know if anything happened to me or his unborn child.

I arrived at the doctor's and had my first exam. K-Dog wasn't able to attend this one but he promised he would be at the rest of them. I would have loved him to be by my side for this first one but duty called.

I started to feel sick again and decided to head back

home instead of going dress shopping. I hadn't checked the mailbox in a few weeks and stopped before going in.

My mailbox was stuffed. I just grabbed all the mail out and went inside. After inside, I sat and chewed on some saltine crackers and sipped ginger ale to soothe my nausea as

I sorted the mail. Most was junk mail, circular flyers and coupons. One letter stood out to me. When I flipped it over it had a big gold seal on it. I picked it up and looked closer. It was actually a government seal. I was puzzled. What could I be receiving from the government? I was not in the mood for and more threatening letters today. I had enough and that bullshit. I ripped the letter open and pulled the contents out.

Inside was a letter of condolences for the death of my husband Deonte. I skimmed the letter and placed the first page down to read what I thought was page two. Instead, my eyes were shocked by the check and the amount of zeros. I was in disbelief. A life insurance check for the death of Deonte in the amount of $200,000 made out to me. My day had somehow turn around. The question now was would I live long enough to enjoy the money. I decided to deposit the check and discuss it with K-Dog later.

...TWENTY...

Richmond had too many bad memories for me so we re-located to Virginia Beach. We were having our wedding at the Founders Inn and I couldn't wait. The place was absolutely beautiful and the perfect place for our wedding. We planned our entire wedding in under a month but not without some challenges. Thank God I had my girls and my family. It was challenging considering I was still having morning sickness and tired all of the time. We didn't want to have a huge party or spend a lot of money, especially when that money could be put towards the businesses we were opening. The idea was for it to be low-key. We even started discussing just going to City Hall but that's what Deonte and I did so I decided against that. We didn't want to make a huge spectacle and have people there who were just being nosy instead of celebrating our new found love.

On that Thursday evening, we were preparing for the rehearsal dinner. It was in one of the banquet halls at the Founders Inn since the wedding and the reception were going to be there also. It just made life easier for me to do everything in one place. Everything was on schedule so you would think that would have my mind at ease but it didn't for two reasons. One, I was still getting threatening phone calls from someone. Two, this was the first time I was meeting K-Dog's mother although we had spoken on the phone a couple of times briefly. Each time we spoke, I could never gauge what her personality was because she was always so serious. If she was anything like Deonte's mom, I was screwed.

As the guests arrived, each one hugged and congratulated me. But you know there's always got to be that one family member that has something to say.

"Where is your husband to be? He didn't run off, did he?" my uncle asked.

I smiled but in my head I was thinking, this mothafucka always got something to say. I wish he would go sit his ass down somewhere and just get drunk like every other Marine does at a gathering where alcohol is served. "He went to pick up his mother from the airport," I said, gritting my teeth.

"Okay, just checking," he said then went to find a seat.

I rolled my eyes and continued to greet guests. A few minutes later, I got a call from a seven-one-eight area code so I assumed K-Dog's phone must've died and he was calling me from his mother's phone.

"Hello," I said excited and turned all the way up.

"So, tomorrow's the big day, huh?"

It was the same voice from the previous calls. "I don't who you are but you're fuckin' with the right one."

"No! You fucked wit' the right one!" the caller screamed.

"Clearly you're scared or you wouldn't let auto tune speak for you. You would just reveal your identity and take me on one-on-one."

"That's what I have planned for tomorrow. We're all going to go out with a bang. You, K-Dog and me. Then we'll all be together again."

"If you come anywhere near me or my family tomorrow you will regret it. I will kill your ass myself!" I yelled.

"Like you've done before, I imagine."

My hands started to shake. My palms were getting sweaty and I felt faint. Everyone who knew about the shootings were dead. I started to think maybe Yaya told someone about the shootings and now they were trying to blackmail me but the caller never asked for money. This was personal. There was a moment when I thought it might be Brina who was stalking me. *Naw, she wouldn't do that after she helped keep Dolo from hurting Zeta,* I thought laughing it off. I hung up the phone and looked around for anyone who didn't belong there. I scanned the room and looked at each and every guest. The sudden tap on my shoulder made me drop my phone. I turned around quickly in a panic.

"I heard you're getting married tomorrow."

"Oh my God! You startled me," I said, scrambled to pick up my phone.

"Ma, this Zsaset. Zsa, this is my mom," K-Dog said smiling.

"Hello, Mrs. Shabazz," I said extending my hand. "It's nice to finally meet you."

"It's Miss Shabazz but you can call me Fatima. You probably should wait before saying it's nice to meet me. You may not be so happy to have met me by the end of the evening," she said firmly.

K-Dog's jaw dropped and my eyes got wide. I was looking for someone to jump out and say it was all a joke, but no one did. All I could do was stand there with this complex look on my face. I didn't know what I was supposed to say so I just said, "That's fair enough. I've heard some really lovely things about you and your work from K-Dog...I mean Kwame."

She looked at her son. "There goes that despicable street name again."

Coley walked up in the knick of time because our first meeting wasn't going well.

"Hey Miss. Fatima. How you doin'," Coley said giving her a hug.

"Hello my brother. I'm doing well. How are you?"

"I'm good."

We were standing there without saying a word for a second. It was so awkward so Coley invited Fatima to go find a table. As soon as they walked away, I whispered to K-Dog, "Oh my God! She hates me already."

185

"No she doesn't. She's just a little upset that the baby won't be brought up as a Muslim."

"Look, we already talked about that. My grandmother, my mother, my kids and I are Baptist. If you want some peace in our household and some more of this good-good, this child is going to grow up Baptist."

"And we have a winner. Baptist it is," he said, putting his arms around my spreading waist.

While we had a few moments to ourselves, I mentioned the phone calls I received. When I saw that K-Dog wasn't taking the call serious, I reminded him how he didn't believe me when I told him about Ra and how that turned out. I shook my head and mumbled a few words to myself.

"I've already hired extra security," he said, kissing me.

"You did?"

"Yep, I knew you were worried about someone messing up our wedding. Now you don't have to worry. You can enjoy our special day."

"Awwww. Thank you baby. I love you."

"I love you more."

The rehearsal dinner went off without incident but I was still on edge. I wasn't if it was just wedding jitters or if it was the threatening calls I was getting. The fact that extra security being there should've calmed my nerves a bit but it didn't. After everyone was gone, K-Dog and I said our goodnights. He was staying on one side of the hotel and I was on the other end. But first, he and his boys were going out to his bachelor party. I reminded him that if he wanted to get a ring put on his finger tomorrow he better be good.

My girls Vicki, Londa and Sheba and I sat in my suite laughing and talking about how different my life was going to be after I got married and the baby was born.

I felt like my old self again and I owed that to K-Dog. Being with him gave me something to be happy about. We talked a little while but then I started to get tired so I excused myself and went to sleep. I could still hear them laughing as I got into bed. Tomorrow was going to be a new beginning and I couldn't wait.

• • •

The wedding day had finally come. Today, Lord willing, I would no longer be Miss Jones. Instead, I was going to be Mrs. Shabazz. We ladies began our day with breakfast and then a stroll around the garden where the ceremony was going to take place. I made sure the guys kept K-Dog in his room. I didn't want to mistakenly see him then have bad luck. The decorations were so beautiful. Our colors were red and white so there were red roses all over the place. I got so emotional just seeing how all of my plans had come into reality. It was everything I envisioned and more.

"Zsa, it's time for you to get dressed girl," Sheba said.

"Okay. Let's do this," I said, rushing towards my room.

We sat in chairs as my talented cousin and her glam squad did our hair and make-up. I decided to wear my hair long and curly. I wanted a relaxed yet romantic look that would go well with the tiara I was wearing. Vicki was dressing Zeta for me. She was going to be the prettiest flower girl ever. We were all talking and trying to get ready when there was a sudden knock at the door that made me jump.

"You okay?" Londa asked.

"Yeah," I replied as Sheba looked to see who it was.

"I hear someone's getting married today."

"Hi mommy! I'm so glad you're here. I want you to help me get dressed," I said excited to see my mom.

"I never thought I would be seeing this day. Especially since I missed the first one."

We all laughed.

"Where's Ryan?" I asked.

"He's with the fellas. He said he didn't want to be around a bunch of girls."

"He says that now but he'll change his mind later," Sheba said laughing.

Once my hair and makeup was done, my mom helped me get into my glamorous empire strapless white dress. I had to buy it two sizes larger because of my belly bump but it still looked great. As I looked at myself in the mirror, I started to shed tears.

"Girl, don't you mess up that slayed make up job," Vicki shouted.

It was too late, so my cousin touched it up.

When the girls got dressed in their red mermaid strapless dresses, we all took photos before we went out to the wedding area. We let Zeta practice her flower throw one more time before we left. She was taking her job a little too seriously for a four year old but we just let her have her way for the day.

"Okay, it's time for us to go." Sheba said.

"Not before I say a prayer," my mom said. We all held hands. "Father God, thank you for this beautiful day. You have fulfilled the desire of our hearts to be together in this life. May we always feel your presence as we sense it throughout this day and may their dedication to one another in marriage be a reflection of your love for everyone in attendance. Defend them from every enemy. Lead them into peace Father God. In the name of Jesus, we pray. Amen."

When we opened our eyes I felt a sense of peace. I walked out of the door with my head held high ready to start my new life with K-Dog. As we were walking down the hall, my brother walked up dressed in his white tux. I told everyone to go ahead of us because we needed a little brother-sister moment. After they walked off, I asked him if he had any information on who was calling me.

"I had my boys check it out but it was a disposable phone."

"I'm scared. I don't want my wedding day to turn into a disaster."

"Don't worry. I have undercover agents mixed in with the guests and I have some posing as servers. Plus, K-Dog has extra security. Everything is going to be fine. I'll be right in the front row," he said, giving me a kiss. "Let's go get you married!"

"Yes! Let's go!"

Before the ceremony started I got to see Ryan in his white tux. Of course, he was our ring bearer.

"Mommy, you look like a princess," Ryan said.

"Awww...thank you baby."

I gave him a smooch and then told him to get into his place. I waited nearby until I was given the cue to walk down the aisle to the altar. I watched as Zeta and Ryan walked down the aisle before me. Seeing them smiling, made me a little emotional so I tried to pull myself together. Moments later, the music changed, signaling me and my brother to walk slowly down the aisle. I remembered walking down the aisle, focused on K-Dog. I don't even remember seeing the guests at that point. When K-Dog and I saw each other for the first time, we both started crying. At the make shift altar, my brother handed me off to my husband to be. We stood and faced one another, the whole time never taking our eyes off of each other. K-Dog held my hand with both of his. We were so excited to be getting married. We were so into the moment it felt like there no one else there.

Our ceremony was going to be short and sweet. There were fun moments, serious moments, and touching moments. There was a prayer, and poem read and then we said our vows. After reading our vows, the minister asked if there was anyone there who felt we shouldn't be joined in marriage. I turned to the guests and gave them the 'I wish a mothafucka would say something look'. Everyone laughed but I was dead serious. Of course, the first person I looked at was K-Dog's mother. She gave me a phony smile but I knew deep down she didn't want him to marry me.

When no one objected, we were pronounced Mr. and Mrs. Shabazz. The preacher told K-Dog he could kiss his bride. I was so relieved.

Maybe the caller was just trying to get under my skin and freak me out so I wouldn't marry K-Dog, I thought.

189

It didn't work. I had a three- carat ring and a diamond encrusted band to prove it. We walked back down the aisle, holding hands and waving at our guests.

A flurry of family photos followed and then it was time to party so we went to the ballroom. A friend of K-Dog's announced us as we walked in and everyone started to clap. The ballroom looked amazing. Our cake was all red velvet. It stood about three feet tall and it looked absolutely beautiful. You could see the 8-tiered cake, the baker created pleats to mimic the pleats on my dress and he used Swarovski crystals appliques to capture the details. The tables were covered in rose petals and the columns were cover in red and white roses. The chairs were covered in white with red sashes.

Before K-Dog and I took our seats at our reception table, my new mother-in-law pulled me to the side.

"Zsaset, I'm sure you're a lovely woman but I'm sorry I do not approve of your union. I think you and my son rushed into this marriage."

I thought that was all she had to say but, oh no…she dropped another bomb on me. She went on to say to me that she felt really uncomfortable lying to all of our guests and talking favorably about our relationship so she wouldn't be making a speech.

I was so happy, not even her words could get under my skin. "Fatima, I'm sorry you feel that way but I do appreciate your honesty and if you don't feel comfortable, you don't have to get up and say anything," I said, then calmly walked over to our DJ and told him that only the best man and my maid of honor would be giving speeches. Problem solved.

After the best man, Coley, and my maid of honor, Sheba, gave their touching speeches, K-Dog and I danced to our song, 'Knocks Me off My Feet' by Stevie Wonder. Mid-way through the song, the kids came out and danced with us. Then everyone else jumped on the dance floor when the DJ played "Candy" by Cameo. It was such a beautiful day and we all were having so much fun.

About three songs in I was tired and I needed to go use the restroom. As I was leaving the dance floor, so was Coley. "Oh no! Where you goin' Zsa? No sittin' down today," Coley said teasing me.

I laughed. "I'm just going to the ladies' room."

"Okay, I gotta go splash some water on my face. I think it's all that expensive champagne I've been drinkin'," he joked.

"Hey, you know Dog had to do it big!"

"True dat."

I walked into the ladies' room and he went into the men's. I had to go into the handicap stall because I needed the extra room.

"Geez, how am I gonna hold up all this material," I said, gathering my dress.

It was a challenge but I was able to use the restroom and not mess up my dress at all. As I was washing my hands, I looked in the mirror. I was so grateful to finally be able to enjoy life after all the hell I had been through. I grabbed a paper towel, dried my hands and headed back to the party.

When I walked out of the door, I got the shock of my life. Before I could yell for help, she pushed me in the men's restroom and locked the door. I was so shaken by her appearance, I almost tripped over Coley's body that was laying on the floor. He had blood coming out of his eyes, mouth and nose.

"Oh my God!" I yelled, as I knelt down beside him. "Coley! Coley! Get up," I yelled. I was too afraid to take my eyes off of her because I didn't know what she was going to do.

"Surprise," she said with the most hateful grin I had ever seen.

I held my stomach and stood up. "What did you do to him?" I said crying.

"What y'all tried to do to me. You do remember, don't you? Or should I show you?"

I started screaming as loud as I could but the music was so loud no one could hear me. *Surely someone has to use the damn bathroom*, I thought.

191

"Scream all you want. No one is gonna come in here because I put an 'out of service' sign up," she said.

I finally paid attention to what she was wearing. She had somehow found a server's outfit and slid right in to the reception. That's when it dawned on me, *that's how she got in here.* I just kept hoping someone would realize I was taking too long and come to look for me. Had I not been six months pregnant, it would've been me and that bitch for sure. I couldn't risk endangering my unborn child so I tried to remain as calm as I could. That was hard to do when I looked down and saw that Coley wasn't moving.

I thought you were dead," I asked not believing my eyes.

"I bet you did. Lucky for me, a crackhead died in the room next to me."

"What?" I asked confused.

"They found a girl dead in the room next to me. The police wanted to see if I heard anything so they knocked on my door. When I didn't answer they assumed I checked out. If the housekeeper hadn't come in when she did I would be dead. I spent months in that damn psychiatric hospital because this mothafucka left a suicide note next to me. But what do y'all care…life went on for y'all. You tried to kill me, mothafucka, now you're gonna die," Lina yelled at Coley.

"We gotta get him some help," I pleaded.

"Fuck him," Lina yelled kicking him. "He tried to kill me. And where is my damn sister," she yelled.

"Lina, I have no idea what you're talking about. The last time we saw Yaya was at O.B's funeral. I swear."

"You're lying!"

"Lina, look at Coley. He needs help."

"K-Dog is probably lookin' like him right about now," she said laughing.

"What?"

"Yeah, I put a little poison in their champagne…well, more than a little," she said, snickering.

"Biiiiitch!" I yelled as I lunged toward her.

We were wrestling all over the bathroom until Coley suddenly jumped up and grabbed her leg. I grabbed the top of the garbage can and hit her with it, then unlocked the door. I was almost out of the door when she grabbed the train of my dress. We were both tugging back and forth but I felt myself about to fall so I turned around and gave my train one hard yank. After I was able to get away from Lina, I ran towards my guests and for one brief moment I thought I was safe until she fired a shot that hit one of my bridesmaids. My guests starting ducking and running for their lives. Everything was moving in slow motion. I tried to scan the room for my kids but I heard another loud pop. I just knew me and my baby were dead until I saw Fatima fighting with one of my guests. She was reaching out and wailing. That's when I turned around and saw K-Dog laying in a pool of blood after jumping in front of a bullet that was meant for me.

"Noooooooooo," I yelled, as I ran to him.

One of my brother's friends tried to wrestle the gun out of Lina's hands before she was able to shoot K-Dog again. As they were wrestling for the gun it went off. It was hard to tell who got hit between Frankie's friend and Lina until she slowly slumped to the floor. My mom hurried my children out of the reception hall to safety as my girls came running over to help me. Frankie reached down to check Lina's pulse but she didn't have one. He walked over to one of the tables, pulled the white tablecloth off and covered Lina's body as a few mortified onlookers watched.

I was fighting and clawing on the floor trying to get next to my husband but they were holding me back. I was laying on the ground on my back with my hand stretched out as my family tried to calm me down. I don't know what they said, I just saw their lips moving. My husband of all of two hours was dying on the floor right next to me. His once crisp white tuxedo was now red. I lost consciousness for a few minutes because when I woke up, they were wheeling him and Coley out of the reception hall.

I felt myself being lifted off the ground, an oxygen mask

being placed over my mouth and the feeling of being wheeled out of the building and into fresh air. I could see my brother running alongside the stretcher while holding my hand. When I looked over and saw the other stretcher being put in the back of the ambulance, I noticed the body wasn't moving. Then I saw a first responded shake his head 'no' to my brother who then looked down at me with tears in his eyes. Everyone was crying and collapsing to the ground and in turn, I immediately lost it. I was so hysterical, I passed out again.

...EPILOGUE...

After being on bed rest in the hospital for a month, I finally gave birth to a beautiful, healthy baby. When I looked back on all of the tragedy and drama I had been through, giving birth was a piece of cake compared to everything else.

"Mommy, is it a boy or girl?" Ryan asked.

"It's a girl! You're a big brother to two sisters," I said.

"Aww man," he said, disappointed it wasn't a boy.

"It's two of us and one of you Ryan," Zeta said, teasing him.

"Don't worry. I got your back." We all turned towards the door and smiled. "We're not gonna let these women take over the house," K-Dog said, limping in the room.

"Me too," Coley said, giving Ryan a high five.

After all the craziness I had been through, I was sitting in my hospital room surrounded by friends and family celebrating the birth of my daughter and married to the one man who had been there for me through it all.

In hindsight, I shoulda' seen it all coming.

Wait...there's more!

ALSO BY DANETTE MAJETTE

CHECK OUT THIS EXCERPT FROM
FILTHY RICH
BY KENDALL BANKS

Dear Diary

Tonight was on the money…The sex was great…The tongue even better. Still…my boo better step up. The stakes are getting higher. He promised to get all my needs fulfilled. It's just not coming fast enough.

Chapter 1

Her build was slim but curvaceous and athletically toned…her stomach washboard smooth. She was the woman most men craved. With long, jet-black, 26" weave draping below her shoulders she seemed perfect...like a sweet, petite goddess. Her light brown skin and thick lips made her assailants second guess their mission. After all, she was supposed to be family.

She was beautiful.

Her beauty couldn't be seen though at this particular moment. It was buried deeply underneath pain, bruises, scars, cuts, blood and tears. She looked nothing like the woman she had always prided herself on being.

Nessa's weave now had no body or shape. It was now heavily matted and dangled wildly over her entire blemished face. Her left eye was swollen and completely shut while her right eye contained semi-blurred vision. Her nose felt like it was broken, making it difficult for her to breathe as blood poured endlessly from both nostrils. Yet she never whined or complained. Her lips were swollen, dry and cracked while blood ran from the slit in her bottom lip. Her fingernails were missing; torturously ripped from her fingers with pliers by her captors. There was absolutely no beauty left to her.

Nessa's body was now as weak as that of a newborn

baby. She had no fight left in her and couldn't stand on her own as the two gunmen dragged her stumbling through the dark woods. Overhead, beams of moonlight dimly illuminated the path in front of them. Her bare feet were becoming more and more soiled with dirt while her sweat soaked her body and clothes. Broken branches snapped underneath them while also piercing her soles so deeply they drew blood, too.

"All you had to do was talk, bitch," one of the goons told her.

He was dressed in a wife beater that exposed his muscular arms covered from wrist to shoulder in gruesome looking scars. Wearing a pair of crispy blue Dickies that sagged his Polo boxers were exposed. On his feet were a pair of white Shell-toed Adidas. In his free hand was a chrome Glock that he intended on using to destroy Nessa for good.

"Yeah, bitch," the gunman on Nessa's left side belted, agreeing with his partner. He was just as muscular as the other man but more thuggish. In his free hand was a black .45 that he'd suddenly decided to press against Nessa's head.

"Got to hand it to you though," he continued. "You're a strong one; real strong. Most bitches fold after only a minute. You got balls, bitch. "

"Hell yeah," the other agreed.

"You though, you hung in there. You went out like a soldier."

Their voices were dripping with sarcasm, not admiration.

Nessa was nearly drifting in and out of consciousness as the men spoke to her. The pain nearly killed her. It was torture. Making her actually wish and yearn for death as she drifted into unconsciousness again. Her mind played back everything from the moment her captors caught her.

The two men had caught Nessa coming out of the hair salon. As she hit the unlock button on the key to her tinted out black Range Rover, a white cargo van emerged out of nowhere and skidded to a stop behind her. Before she could react its side door slid open and two masked men jumped out. In the blink of an eye they had her in their arms with a hand over her mouth and tossed her inside. The next several hours were the most brutal and terrifying she'd ever experienced or endured.

"Where the fuck Luke's stash houses at?" was one of the questions Nessa was asked over and over again.

"Fuck you!" she returned countless times, even spitting in one of the captors' face once when he got too close.

Nessa wasn't weak. She wasn't soft. She had a past full of violence and had crazy survival skills. She'd been born and bred to be loyal. The term "Death Before Dishonor" meant something special to her. She even had it tattooed in old English letters across her bikini line. For her, those words weren't just a phrase. They were a way of life, especially when it came to the most important man in her life...

Luke.

Luke and his family were the most successful crime family Washington D.C. had ever seen. They were a family of multimillionaires who ran each of their enterprises with an iron fist. Disrespect wasn't tolerated. Fear among their soldiers wasn't accepted. Talking to the police was a mandatory death sentence.

They weren't a joke.

Nessa was Luke's heart. She was both his queen and princess. He kept a plush roof over her head and her pockets loaded. The rare diamonds around her wrists and neck couldn't be rivaled by many. Luke had real money...old and new. He kept the most expensive clothes and fabrics on Nessa's skin and the newest designer heels and sandals on her pedicured feet.

He loved her but beyond measure.

It was because of that love that Nessa would never tell on him or his family. She didn't care who was asking. It didn't matter if those infiltrators were killers or the Feds themselves. She'd die before turning over on Luke. And during the current moment, it looked like dying was exactly what she was going to do.

For hours in the dirty basement that smelled of mildew and piss, the torture and abuse continued. As a light bulb dangled by a thin wire from overhead, she was beaten, choked, slapped, kicked and spat on. All of it occurred as she sat helpless in a wooden chair with her wrists and ankles duct taped to it.

"Talk, bitch!" one of the men yelled just before punching her in the face so hard she thought her jaw was broken. "Where the fuck his stash houses at?"

Dazed and barely able to lift her chin from her breasts, she said weakly, "Eat a dick, bitch!"

Looking at his partner, the goon laughed and said, "Whoaaaaaaaaaaa, she's got balls. Eat a dick, huh?"

With her chin in her chest and looking up at him through her matted hair and swollen eye, she said, "What, you deaf, muthafucka? Yeah, I said eat a dick."

The two men laughed again. One of them then unzipped his pants, freed his dick and said, "Naw, bitch. How 'bout you drink some piss?" He then began to urinate all over her. By the time he was finished, piss had drenched her weave and tank top. Its stench smelled so bad she threw up all over the floor.

"We can do this all night, bitch," he told her as he placed his dick back in his pants and zipped up. "I don't have any place to be. And you just might get raped in this muthufucka if you don't talk soon."

Several moments passed by. Nessa feared getting raped but still remained silent. Soon, more punches battered Nessa's face.

"Talk, hoe!" the gunman demanded as he struck _ ____
in the stomach.

*Coughing and gasping for air, Nessa said, "Okay,
okay, I'll...I'll..."*

"You'll what?" he asked, pressing his ear close to her
face.

"I'll talk," she told him. "I...I promise, I'll talk."

*Looking at his partner with a grin, he said, "Alright,
bitch, talk. Tell us what we want to hear. Tell us where the
fuck Luke keeps all that bread."*

*With pain and torment evident in her voice, she told
him, "The...the...the next time...I'm..."*

Both men listened carefully.

*"The next time...I'm...I'm on my period, eat my bloody
pussy, bitch ass nigga. How's that? Is that what your soft ass
wanted to hear?" She then laughed wildly. Her ribs ached
terribly. But she forced the laughter.*

*Growing infuriated, the goon punched her twice. "You
think this is a game, bitch? You think we're playing?" He
pulled his gun out and prepared to pistol whip her until his
partner stopped him.*

Instead...More punches.

*After several minutes, he said, "Alright, I've got some-
thing for you." He then pulled a pair of pliers from his back
pocket.*

Nessa weakly raised her throbbing head to see them.

"Let's see if this gets you to talk."

*The man then latched the mouth of the pliers to the
nail of Nessa's forefinger and began to pull until it ripped
from its roots.*

*Nessa screamed at the top of her lungs in pain. Tears
flowed from her eyes as she breathed heavily.*

"Talk, bitch!"

She formed an even more stern face yet stayed silent as the tears continued to flow.

Another nail was ripped from her hand. She screamed even louder than before. The pain was unbearable. She'd never felt anything so excruciating.

"Where the fucking money at? Just tell us about one stash house and we'll let you live."

"Fuck you, muthafucka. Kill me!" she shouted.

Another slap.

Another punch.

"Kill me," she screamed. "Kill me, muthafuckas. And after you do, kill yourselves. Because when Luke finds out what you've done there won't be a place on earth your scum ass will be able to hide!"

With an open hand she was smacked viciously and knocked to the ground.

The slap brought Nessa back to current reality…still in the dark, creepy woods. The men now had her between them as they stood at what looked like a freshly dug grave. She was too weak to raise her head and didn't want to open her useable eye.

"Pay attention, bitch," the gunman who'd slapped her ordered. "This is the good part. You don't want to miss your own damn funeral, do you?"

From over the pit, Nessa looked down into it to see an opened casket sitting at the bottom. Inside the casket was a body covered in blood. Its eyes were open and staring directly up at her. Nessa immediately panicked.

Feeling and sensing her fear, both men laughed.

"Don't worry 'bout him, baby girl," one of them said. "We just put his ass in there to keep you company. He ain't gon' bite. He dead already."

They laughed again.

"Alright, bitch, last chance," she was told. "You want

to tell us where those stash houses are? That's all it takes. Tell us what we want; we let you go 'bout your business."

Silently, Nessa saw Luke's face in her head. She heard his voice. All his motivational words…his loving words. She felt his kisses. She remembered the first time they met. She remembered their love making. She knew exactly where he kept most of his money and where his major stash houses were located. She could easily reveal the details and live. But each thought and memory made her tell her captors one final time…

"Fuck you."

She refused to turn on her man.

Shaking their heads, both men said almost at the exact same time, "Suit yourself then. You's a dead bitch, now."

With those words said, she was shoved into the pit and into the casket. Her body crashed down on the chest of the dead man as she screamed loudly.

"Noooooooooooo! Fuck Nooooooo! Don't do thissssssssss!"

She and he were now eye to eye. Her insides shook and bile rose up in her gut.

The casket shut.

Nessa vomited once again.

Darkness dominated.

Nessa, although hardened by the many things she'd experienced in life, broke down. She'd been taught to survive through several foster homes, abduction, family deaths, and violence at the hand of an old love, but nothing to this extreme. She couldn't help sobbing as she heard the dirt crashing down on the roof of the casket. Knowing she was going to be buried alive had her body shaking and her heart pounding.

As moment after moment passed by, she thought about Luke. She was dying inside knowing she'd never see him again. She wished she could tell him she loved him one last time. She wished she could kiss him one more time. She wished he had come to his senses and agreed to marry her before now.

More dirt crashed down.

Seconds seemed like hours.

Besides the vomit, the blood of the dead man underneath her turned her stomach. She could smell it. In fact, it wasn't a *smell*. It was a stench. It sickened her terribly. She wanted to cover her nostrils but her arms were far too weak. She could only lay there.

And wait to die.

A slow death.

Moments passed.

More dirt crashing down sounded.

More moments passed.

Suddenly…

Silence.

Nessa wondered why the sound of falling dirt had ceased. She listened closely. She could hear voices but couldn't make out what they were saying.

Then more silence.

Then…

The casket opened.

A shot gun was now in sight.

Moonlight immediately flooded the pit. Nessa, still in the most pain she'd ever experienced in her life, mustered up the strength to raise her head from the dead man's chest. Slightly, she turned to look toward the top of the pit. What she saw staring down at her both frightened and confused her…

Those eyes.

Those green eyes.

Was it really him?

Chapter 2

The tinted black S550 Mercedes Benz gracefully slithered through D.C. a little after one a.m. Underneath the night's full moon and glistening stars, the luxury whip passed by war-torn, battered-beyond-repair neighborhoods. Vacant buildings, lots and store fronts lined main streets. Abandoned houses, unkempt lawns, and busted out streetlamps lined side streets. The neighborhoods were a far cry from the city's bustling and brightly lit downtown. The west side seemed like the land that time forgot.

Despite the time of night, the neighborhood's worst of the worst and most disappointing roamed its streets and sidewalks. Crackheads and prostitutes walked the shadows on missions to find money to feed their drug habits. Their faces and bodies showed the ravaging consequences of years of addiction and abuse. Dope boys, most young and strapped with guns, stood on corners anxious to sell them the poison they chased endlessly day and night. From distances not too far away gunshots echoed along with blaring police sirens.

From the back seat of the Benz and from behind the darkness of the windows' tint, Luke stared out at the ghetto's hopeless and violent landscape in thought, knowing he was a huge reason why the entire city's black community had fallen into such turmoil. It was mainly the Heroin from his family's multimillion dollar Cocaine and Meth drug ring that flowed through their veins. It was his family's crack and marijuana that flooded their lungs. It was his family's guns that countless gangsters, including children, clutched while playing their part in running up the city's overwhelming murder rate.

Luke's family was undoubtedly the most successful family of kingpins Washington D.C. had seen since Rayful Edmonds. They hadn't achieved their success through only violence, intimidation and murder though. They'd also achieved it by building relationships and alliances with folks in high places. They had a man in the DEA. They had police officers on the take. They had a judge in their pocket. They were even due a few favors from the city's mayor because they had been a huge reason why the mayor won the election in the first place. During Mayor Walberg's campaign and electoral race, their family threatened and bullied voters into voting for him. The family also contributed thousands of dollars to the mayor's campaign. The assistance and influence resulted in a landslide win.

As Luke stared out of the car's window at the world around him, he felt more like a prisoner of his family's success than anything else. He felt more like a failure than an accomplished business man.

He felt like a criminal.

Somehow he hated the wealthy life and the past that led him to his current position. His family held so many secrets that most would puke, cry, and run for the hills if they got wind of what was taking place. Luke dropped his head and looked down at Nessa's battered and bruised face as it lay in his lap. Her eyes were closed. He grimaced at the sight as he began to rub her head softly. His eyes slowly roamed from her face down the entire length of her body. He saw bruises, cuts and blood. His nostrils smelled the stench of the blood and urine. He was sickened but not by what he saw. No; what sickened him was the part he himself had played in her assault.

Luke had given the order.

It nearly destroyed Luke when he ordered his goons to test the loyalty of the woman he loved. Nessa was his lady, his ride or die, his bitch; his number one. It shattered his heart in countless pieces to have to give such an order. But just like so many other things he despised during his life in this business, it had to be done. He had no choice but to accept it and hope she would still love him afterward. He had to be sure Nessa wasn't the insider feeding information to those after him.

Against his brother's fears, Luke had begun sharing private information about the family business over the last few months. He'd told her where he kept large sums of cash. She knew about a few of the stash houses. She knew workers, lawyers, contacts, and most of all, family secrets. Looking down at Nessa, Luke realized he'd made a good decision by trusting her.

The Mercedes turned off of a main street and into a dark alley. As the car's tires made their way down the alley's trash cluttered pavement, its headlight's brought into view a parked Cadillac Escalade. Two men were sitting inside; one in the driver's seat, the other in the passenger seat. Both goons had been the two who had inflicted Nessa's torture on her. After they dumped her in the makeshift grave, Luke sent them to handle crew business and then meet him here.

The brakes of the Benz's factory rimmed wheels squealed lightly as the car came to an abrupt stop. After placing the whip in park, the driver stepped out and began to make his way along the passenger side towards the trunk and around to Luke's door. When he reached the door, he opened it graciously.

Luke eased his thigh from underneath Nessa's head

and replaced it with the palm of his hand as he slid out of the backseat. With his hand he lovingly rested her head down on the seat. He then took off his suit jacket revealing a shoulder holster and gun. His once white dress shirt was now stained in Nessa's blood. The thighs of his pants were also. He softly placed the suit coat over her. A moment later he slipped his hands into a pair of plastic gloves.

Nessa, still dazed from her beating, mumbled something incoherently to Luke. "Shhhhhhh," he said, placing his lips to her ear softly. "I'll be back shortly. I promise." He then kissed her on the cheek affectionately and shut the door.

Stuffing his hands into the pockets of his pants, Luke and his driver headed towards the Escalade. Behind them, The Mercedes's headlights shined illuminating the area between them and the SUV. As they walked, the heels of Luke's fourteen hundred dollar, Tom Ford loafers clicked and echoed off the walls of the abandoned buildings lining both sides of the narrow alleyway. The two men awaiting them in the SUV climbed out. Both groups of men met up in front of the Escalade's hood.

"The two of you did an exceptional job tonight," Luke commended them while still keeping his hands in his pockets. "You do good work."

Both goons looked at each other and smiled proudly, glad that their work was to their bossman's liking. Everyone wanted to please Luke at all times, no matter the cost.

"I appreciate that," Luke told them.

"It was nothin'," one of the men replied. "Whatever you need done, you know we're always game for that shit."

"Really?" Luke asked, glaring at the huge gap between his teeth.

"That's right, boss."

"Even if I ordered you to smoke our boy here?"

The man turned to his partner with a sinister stare.

Then looked back at Luke.

The moment became far too weird.

"It's all business, right?" he asked Luke then shrugged his shoulders.

Luke nodded. He then looked at his driver and said, "Pay these soldiers. They've done what I asked."

The driver reached into his suit jacket's inner pocket, pulled out an envelope and handed it to one of the goons. The goon didn't even bother to open it. With a smile on his face, he simply stuffed it in the front pocket of his jeans.

"You're not going to count it?" Luke asked.

"Nahhhh, you're good. We trust you."

"Important rule, gentlemen; never trust anyone."

The goons nodded.

With that said, Luke turned to head back to the Benz. His driver did also. After taking several steps, Luke stopped, turned and said as if he'd forgotten something, "Oh, gentlemen, one other thing?"

The two goons were heading around the hood of the Escalade as he spoke. They stopped and turned to him. "What's up, boss?"

Luke pulled his hands from his pockets, grabbed the gun from his holster, took aim at the man on the truck's driver side and squeezed the trigger.

Amidst the gun's thundering blast, its bullet tore through the man's forehead and ripped the entire back of his skull off. Brain, skull and patches of hair scattered on the ground and the Escalade's driver's side door. The man crumpled to the ground.

"What the fuck?" the man on the passenger side said in surprise and disbelief. Fear quickly captured his entire face as his eyes went from where his partner was once standing to Luke.

Luke immediately took aim at him. With one last glare

into the gap between his teeth he sighed. "Respect is everything."

Raising his hands in defense, his eyes wide, the goon asked, "What did I do?"

Without giving him an answer, Luke squeezed the trigger again. The back of the man's head exploded just like his partner's had done. He hit the ground a second later. Luke then walked over to the first man and stood over him. Blood spilled from the back of his skull and flowed endlessly. Luke, unfazed by the blood, let off three shots in the man's chest to insure he was dead. As he did, each shot was accompanied by bright flashes from the gun. Empty shell casings spilled from the side of the barrel onto the ground. Immediately after the last shot was fired, he headed around the hood to the second man. Seeing him lying on his back with half his head gone and his legs twitching, Luke fired three shots into his chest. The man's body went totally still.

Silence.

Brief moments passed.

Luke turned and walked back to his driver. The driver didn't say anything. He'd seen countless men murdered in this business, the game his employer was in. This one wasn't expected though. There had been no forewarning. Instead of saying a word though, he only looked at Luke with a sort of bewildered stare. Knowing what the driver wanted to ask, Luke said to him, "No man should know how it feels to harm another man's woman and live."

With those words said, Luke handed the handle of the gun to the driver and said, "Get rid of the gun and the bodies. I'll drive myself home."

Taking off the rubber gloves, Luke headed to the Benz.

Order Your Copy of
Filty Rich
Today!!

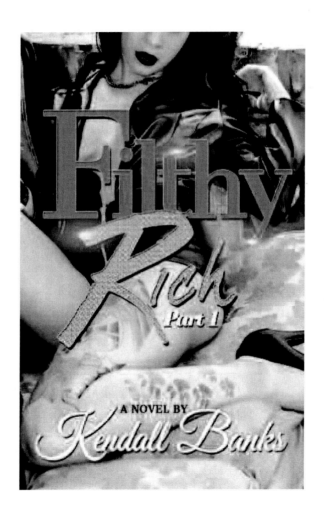

HERE'S MORE EXCERPTS FROM
LIFE CHANGING BOOKS...

HEART BREAKER
BY: BRIANA COLE

One

Some men were just too damn easy, it was almost pathetic. Jayla licked her lips as she watched him approach her. She had to admit though, he was much better looking than his fiancée had described. She watched his thick lips curl in an approving smile as his fingers stroked the smooth cut of his goatee. Hershey chocolate skin, muscles rippling through the black T-shirt, and a wide, confident walk like his dick was too damn big for his jeans. She would be the judge of that soon enough.

"Excuse me," he said. "I don't mean to bother you, but you are damn sure the finest woman in this bar tonight."

She returned his smile with a seductive one of her own. He probably wouldn't feel that way if he knew his fiancée, Tracy, was shadowed in the DJ booth. Jayla could almost feel her calculating eyes watching their every move.

Jayla crossed her legs, allowing the slit of the fire-red dress to inch up. As if on cue, his eyes dipped to the exposed piece of her chocolate thigh and she felt her pussy heat in response. She ran her manicured fingers through the black tresses of the wig. "Thank you," she said. "And you are?"

"Marcus."

Bold one to use his real name, Jayla thought as she took a sip from her drink.

"And you are?" he prompted when she intentionally made no move to speak again.

Jayla winked. "Very interested in you, Marcus," she said.

"Is that so?"

"You damn right," she said, standing. Her titties were nearly spilling out of the low V-shape neckline and she boldly pressed them against his solid chest. The gesture stroked her nipples until they hardened between them. She leaned up until her cheek grazed his, her lips a whisper from his ear.

"I would absolutely love to dance with you," she said and slowly licked her lips, making sure the tip of her tongue touched his earlobe in the process. Not bothering to wait for his response, she slid past him and made her way to the dance floor.

The slow reggae mix had a collection of slick bodies grinding and swaying in the multi-colored glow of the strobe lights. Jayla maneuvered through the crowd; a mixture of musk, perfume, and alcohol so thick it was nearly edible. She felt Marcus's arm circle her waist and pull her body to his. She pressed her back against him, leaned her head on his shoulder and began rocking her hypnotic hips to the beat.

She let her body take over, gyrating her ass against him until the prominent bulge in his pants tightened. When he placed his hands on her waist, she put her hands on top of his and gripped his fingers. Slowly, she guided them up to cup her titties and heard his accepting moan muffled against her hair.

He used his thumbs to massage her nipples until they pierced the satin material. He began to jab his hips forward, his dick straining against the thick material as he thrust it, repeatedly, against her ass.

Jayla wiggled against him, pleased when she saw his eyes had drifted closed. Sheer pleasure mirrored his face, his mouth hanging slightly open. He was good and ready. And judging by the heated moisture dampening the crotch of her thongs, so was she.

Tracy had made the instructions clear in the contract—take him as far as he would allow. Hopefully, he knew how to put it down so she could at least get some satisfaction.

"I hope I'm not being too forward," she whispered, a combination of liquor and practice giving her voice a sexual rasp. "But I've got a case of Coronas in my fridge that I would hate to see go to waste. Why don't you follow me home so I can...give it to you, Marcus?"

"I would hate to waste good beer," he said.

Jayla took his hand and headed towards the door. This part was always difficult for the women to watch. She'd even had one client storm up to her on their way out; the combination of sobs, curses, and strong Spanish accent rendering the woman completely incomprehensible. If this one interfered, Jayla would politely back off as agreed. Her clients were always aware upfront that even if they stopped the evaluation before it was completed, the payment was the same.

As soon as they stepped outside, she opened her mouth to speak and gasped when he dragged her towards him. She didn't have time to process a reaction before his other hand grabbed the back of her neck and crushed his lips against hers.

She tasted the lingering Corona on his tongue, felt the urgency in the kiss as his hand lowered to squeeze her ass. He seemed to be trying to mesh their bodies together, his package taut against her leg. She flicked her tongue on the roof of his mouth before taking a step back.

"Soon," she said. She then turned on her heel and headed to her SUV. He was at her side in two strides and Jayla gasped when he grabbed her arm again and whirled her around to face him once more.

"Can't wait," he said, his voice thick. He took her hand and placed it on his dick. "You feel this shit? I need your ass now."

Jayla bit her lip, pretending to consider the proposition. Luckily, she had the tape recorder already rolling in the truck.

She had to admit, Tracy's request for a tape recording was strange, but she obliged. Some just needed hard evidence. As if it would make a difference.

"I'm parked over here." She tipped her head toward the darkened SUV, the crisp, black paint and tinted windows glistening in the stream of moonlight.

Jayla hadn't even completely closed the door on the backseat before Marcus attacked her body. She bit back a curse as she heard the rip of satin; then winced when she felt the sudden bite of air on her exposed skin. The hair on his face scratched her breast as he devoured. He polished her nipple, flicking his tongue, licking and sucking until it was hard and nearly dripping wet.

"Yes, please fuck me Marcus." Her words came out in an anxious breath. She scooted to lie back on the chilled leather, spreading her knees to welcome him. Her panties were already stained with her pre-juices as she rubbed them against her pussy lips. She nudged the flimsy material to the side and stroked her swelling clit, giggling to herself when she saw his eyes dancing in anticipation.

"Oh yeah, Baby, I'm gone fuck the shit outta you." His breath was coming out jagged and rough as he fumbled with his pants.

Jayla dipped her fingers inside her sugar walls, allowing her nectar to spill onto her finger. As he watched, she lifted her finger to her mouth and sucked it clean. "Baby, don't you want to sample it first?" she teased.

He nodded and dove in, his tongue thrashing over her clit. His slurping noises echoed in the car as he put his lips to her hole and attempted to fuck her with his tongue.

Jayla frowned, swallowing her disappointment. His tongue was the size of his hand but he damn sure didn't know how to work it. It was much too wild and messy for her. But oh well. It wasn't like he was her man. So, she moaned and grinded against his mouth like he was eating her to kingdom come.

"Yes, yes," she exaggerated, allowing her flavor to coat his taste buds. "Eat that shit Marcus. Eat your pussy, Baby."

When she faked her orgasm, he sat up and pulled his dick from his boxers. Jayla took the condom from him and with the fingers of an expert, ripped open the package. The sound of the crinkling latex had her smiling as the material stretched over his erection. No, size was not an issue at all. Swinging her leg over his lap to straddle his waist, she lowered herself slowly to savor each generous inch and watched the rapid succession of emotions play on his face.

She started slow, clenching and releasing her pussy muscles in a massaging technique and moaning as if his size was unbearable. She leaned over so her body rested on his and felt his desperate clutch to keep her positioned.

The thick heat had coated the inside of the car; fog permeating to haze the windows. She even tasted the faint hint of sweat as she licked his neck. When his eyes rolled back, she quickened her pace and bounced her ass even harder. She felt the throb of his dick as he

218

braced for the anticipated orgasm.

"Oh shit," he all but yelled as he came, lifting his body from the seat with the force of his release.

He sighed as Jayla slowed to a stop, laughing to herself. *Was that all? Damn, that was a quick $10,000.*

She didn't even bother lingering. Just lifted off and moved to settle on the seat beside him. She blew out a breath, feeling the first beads of sweat dot her forehead under the synthetic hair of the wig. Now to get him out without all that extra shit.

"Damn, Girl," he said, eyeing the filled condom. "You got some good stuff."

Jayla smiled as she smoothed her dress back in place. He had ripped it on the side, so the hole did little to cover her plump breasts. She sighed, already knowing she and Tara would have to get back out to the mall so she could get another. It was one of her favorites.

"You were great, Marcus," she said, sneaking a glance at the digital clock on her dashboard. "I definitely needed that."

The ego stroke had him grinning like he'd just won the lottery. "Anytime. You keep giving me that ass like you just did, I'm all yours."

Jayla watched him slide the condom off and fold it back into the wrapper. "You got a girlfriend Marcus?" she asked.

Silence.

He lifted his shoulder in a half shrug as if pretending to be totally engrossed in the act of pulling up his pants. He mumbled something to the effect of 'not really' and had Jayla rolling her eyes. Of course not. He had a fiancée which was even worse. The wedding was in two weeks but, of course, she wasn't supposed to know that. *A dog, through and through.*

"I got someone I'm talking to," he went on. "But she don't mean nothing. She definitely ain't as fine as you." He leaned in and used his index finger to trace her lips. "Besides, I would rather get to know you better."

Jayla nodded and reaching to the front seat, grabbed the pen and scratch paper she had placed in the cup holder. She scribbled a fake number on the paper before kissing it and handing it to him.

"Call me," she whispered.

He planted another kiss on her lips before opening the door. "Most definitely," he said. "I think I'm in love." He laughed at his own joke before shutting the door.

Jayla released a disgusted breath. The trifling bastard didn't even know her name. Pa-fucking-thetic. Tracy would be lucky to get rid of him. If she got rid of him.

Jayla climbed into the driver's seat. Reaching under the steering wheel, she stopped the recorder. She said 'if', because the woman seemed desperate, naïve, and downright dumb enough to stay with the man even when she knew the truth. Jayla figured the evidence wouldn't matter one bit.

The sudden bang on her passenger window had Jayla screaming. She squinted through the tinted glass and let out an aggravated sigh when she recognized Tracy's tight-lipped frown, brooding hazel eyes, and inches of weave hiked in a hasty ponytail. *What the hell?*

Before Jayla could lock the doors, Tracy slid into the front seat and Jayla looked to the back when she heard another door open. Tracy's sister, Lauren, jumped in looking pissed and frowning at the wet stains on the leather seats.

"What the fuck are you two doing here?" Panic had Jayla shouting the question as she snatched her wig off, letting her mane of auburn hair spring free.

Tracy sniffed the air and frowned at the distinct odor. "So, I guess you fucked him, huh?"

"Hell yeah they fucked," Lauren's voice was laced with a bitter angriness. "Can't you tell? Shit, it smells like nothing but ass in this car. I told you that nigga wasn't shit, Tracy."

Unsatisfied, Tracy starred at Jayla, her eyes tight with hurt and restrained anger of her own. "Did you fuck him?"

"What the hell do you think?" Jayla snapped, rolling her eyes. "Isn't that what you paid me to do? Fuck him? Or have you forgotten our little contract?"

"Tracy, let's beat this nasty bitch," Lauren yelled.

"Beat me? For what?" Jayla looked from Lauren, bouncing on the edge of her seat in anticipation, to Tracy who just sat eyeing her in silence. "I just saved you from making a big ass mistake by showing you what kind of lying sack of shit you were about to marry. I just proved your nigga ain't shit so what the fuck you questioning me for? Y'all need to be thanking me."

Silence. Jayla smirked as Tracy sat hunched in the seat like a whipped puppy. She was almost as pathetic as her man. "I don't know why you're pissed," Jayla went on. "He can't fuck or eat pussy so y'all lucky I'm not charging extra for wasting my damn time."

Tracy's slap carried enough force to throw Jayla backwards. She winced, partially from the sting of her cheek and partially from the impact of her arm as it slammed against the door. Fuming, Jayla lunged towards Tracy, prepared to fight Lauren off and punch them both through the damn window. She stopped short when Tracy burst into hysterical sobs.

"I'm sorry." Tracy buried her face in her hands. "I just can't believe he did this to me. I loved that bastard."

Jayla pursed her lips, still seething from the slap. It was time for these crazy bitches to leave. She snatched the recorder from under the steering wheel and dropped it on the seat beside Tracy. "Consider this my final report," she said. "Give me my damn money and get the fuck outta my car."

Tracy's face was tear-stricken as she gazed at the tape recorder. She sighed. "Lauren, give her the money and let's go."

Lauren smacked her lips and pulled an envelope from her Coach purse. "Take it then, you trashy bitch," she said as she snatched the crisp bills from the envelope and threw them in Jayla's face. Money rained down to pool in Jayla's lap and litter the floor. "And we better not see your ass on the street or we gone fuck you up. Believe that, you skanky bitch." Lauren got out of the car and slammed the door behind her.

Tracy glared at Jayla as she grabbed the recorder. "I hope it was worth it for you." Her voice had lowered to something almost sinister as she stared a moment or two longer.

Jayla narrowed her eyes. Fear was beginning to inch its way up her spine. "Get away from me," she whispered through clenched teeth.

Without another word, Tracy climbed from the car and shut the door.

Jayla waited until both sisters had crossed the parking lot before she let out a staggered breath of relief. She looked in the rearview mirror and saw her heavy eye makeup had begun to smear and her cheek had colored to a light red from the hit. Jayla rolled her eyes. She could almost bank that even after all the theatrics, Tracy would still probably say 'I do' to be Mrs. Marcus Harris.

Oh well. She had done her job and gotten paid for it. Everything afterwards had nothing to do with her.

A quick flash of light had Jayla squinting through her windshield. *Had someone taken a picture of her?* She scrunched her face in confusion, eyeing the seemingly empty row of cars lined in front. Her eyes met the darkness and she had to swallow a bit of uneasiness.

Flipping the car in drive, Jayla peeled out of the space, concluding she had indulged in one too many drinks. Wondering if she would call her playmate for some *real* dick, Jayla didn't even realize the second flash from the camera, briefly illuminating the 'TRU BAIT' letters etched in her license plate.

Heart Breaker...In Stores Now

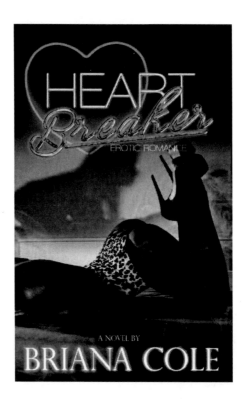

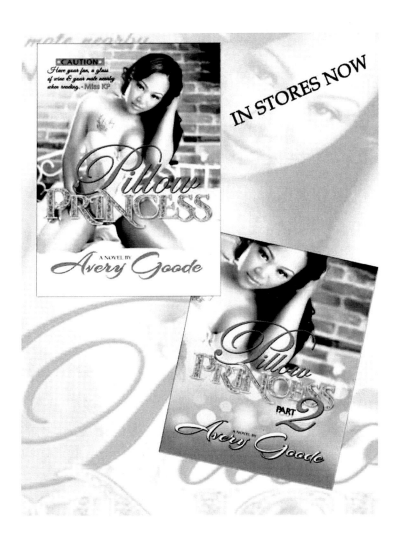

CHECK OUT THESE LCB SEQUELS

LCB BOOK TITLES

See More Titles At
www.lifechangingbooks.net

ORDER FORM

MAIL TO:
PO Box 423
Brandywine, MD 20613
301-362-6508

Ship to:

Address:

Date: Phone:

Email: City & State: Zip:

Make all money orders and cashiers checks payable to: **Life Changing Books**

Qty.	ISBN	Title	Release Date	Price
	0-9741394-2-4	Bruised by Azarel	Jul-05	$ 15.00
	0-9741394-7-5	Bruised 2: The Ultimate Revenge by Azarel	Oct-06	$ 15.00
	0-9741394-3-2	Secrets of a Housewife by J. Tremble	Feb-06	$ 15.00
	0-9741394-6-7	The Millionaire Mistress by Tiphani	Nov-06	$ 15.00
	1-934230-99-5	More Secrets More Lies by J. Tremble	Feb-07	$ 15.00
	1-934230-95-2	A Private Affair by Mike Warren	May-07	$ 15.00
	1-934230-96-0	Flexin & Sexin Volume 1	Jun-07	$ 15.00
	1-934230-89-8	Still a Mistress by Tiphani	Nov-07	$ 15.00
	1-934230-91-X	Daddy's House by Azarel	Nov-07	$ 15.00
	1-934230-88-X	Naughty Little Angel by J. Tremble	Feb-08	$ 15.00
	1-934230820	Rich Girls by Kendall Banks	Oct-08	$ 15.00
	1-934230839	Expensive Taste by Tiphani	Nov-08	$ 15.00
	1-934230782	Brooklyn Brothel by C. Stecko	Jan-09	$ 15.00
	1-934230669	Good Girl Gone bad by Danette Majette	Mar-09	$ 15.00
	1-934230707	Sweet Swagger by Mike Warren	Jun-09	$ 15.00
	1-934230677	Carbon Copy by Azarel	Jul-09	$ 15.00
	1-934230723	Millionaire Mistress 3 by Tiphani	Nov-09	$ 15.00
	1-934230715	A Woman Scorned by Ericka Williams	Nov-09	$ 15.00
	1-934230685	My Man Her Son by J. Tremble	Feb-10	$ 15.00
	1-924230731	Love Heist by Jackie D.	Mar-10	$ 15.00
	1-934230812	Flexin & Sexin Volume 2	Apr-10	$ 15.00
	1-934230748	The Dirty Divorce by Miss KP	May-10	$ 15.00
	1-934230758	Chedda Boyz by CJ Hudson	Jul-10	$ 15.00
	1-934230766	Snitch by VegasClarke	Oct-10	$ 15.00
	1-934230693	Money Maker by Tonya Ridley	Oct-10	$ 15.00
	1-934230774	The Dirty Divorce 2 by Miss KP	Nov-10	$ 15.00
	1-934230170	The Available Wife by Carla Pennington	Jan-11	$ 15.00
	1-934230774	One Night Stand by Kendall Banks	Feb-11	$ 15.00
	1-934230278	Bitter by Danette Majette	Feb-11	$ 15.00
	1-934230299	Married to a Balla by Jackie D.	May-11	$ 15.00
	1-934230308	The Dirty Divorce Part 3 by Miss KP	Jun-11	$ 15.00
	1-934230316	Next Door Nympho By CJ Hudson	Jun-11	$ 15.00
	1-934230286	Bedroom Gangsta by J. Tremble	Sep-11	$ 15.00
	1-934230340	Another One Night Stand by Kendall Banks	Oct-11	$ 15.00
	1-934230359	The Available Wife Part 2 by Carla Pennington	Nov-11	$ 15.00
	1-934230332	Wealthy & Wicked by Chris Renee	Jan-12	$ 15.00
	1-934230375	Life After a Balla by Jackie D.	Mar-12	$ 15.00
	1-934230251	V.I.P. by Azarel	Apr-12	$ 15.00
	1-934230383	Welfare Grind by Kendall Banks	May-12	$ 15.00
	1-934230413	Still Grindin' by Kendall Banks	Sep-12	$ 15.00
	1-934230391	Paparazzi by Miss KP	Oct-13 *	$ 15.00
	1-93423043X	Cashin' Out by Jai Nicole	Nov-12	$ 15.00
	1-934230634	Welfare Grind Part 3 by Kendall Banks	Mar-13	$15.00
	1-934230642	Game Over by Winter Ramos	Apr-13	$15.99
	1-934230618	My Counterfeit Husband by Carla Pennington	Aug-14	$ 15.00
	1-93423060X	Mistress Loose by Kendall Banks	Oct-13	$ 15.00
	1-934230626	Dirty Divorce Part 4	Jan-14	$ 15.00
	1-934230596	Left for Dead by Ebony Canion	Feb-14	$ 15.00
	1-934230456	Charm City by C. Flores	Mar-14	$ 15.00
	1-934230499	Pillow Princess by Avery Goode	Aug-14	$ 15.00
			Total for Books	$

* Prison Orders- Please allow up to three (3) weeks for delivery.

Shipping Charges (add $4.95 for 1-4 books*) $

Total Enclosed (add lines) $